Berringden Brow

On Days Like These

Jill Robinson

Berringden Books

Published 2021 by Berringden Books
berringdenbrow@hotmail.co.uk
Revised edition 2023
copyright Jill Robinson 2023

This is a work of fiction and identification of any character with any living person should not be inferred.

All rights reserved

The right of Jill Robinson to be identified as the author of this work has been asserted in accordance with the Copyright designs and Patents Act 1988

ISBN0-95464000-7-1

Cover illustration: Hannah Bunn: hannahbunn@hotmail.co.uk

For Dorota

Chapter 1

It seemed to Jess that half the village was assembled on Berringden Brow park that warm September evening. The sunny weather had continued well into the autumn, even here in the high Pennines, and everyone was making the most of it. People were gathered around disposable barbecues, cooking sausages and steaks, drinking cans of beer or bottles of Prosecco and screaming with laughter while the meat turned to burnt offerings; meanwhile, depending on age and inclination, their children played football, climbed on the adventure playground, threw rubbish into the pond or lurked behind the bushes, furtively smoking. The distinctive smell of marijuana drifted through the air, competing with the barbecue smoke. Music blared from rival speakers and half a dozen capering dogs scrapped and barked wildly at the prospect of the food soon to be thrown their way.

Jess was peripheral to this joyful scene, being happy simply to observe the merriment from among the blackberry bushes where she was steadily picking. She had left her own dog, a Staffy named Izzy, at home, in order to be able to concentrate on her fruit gathering free from the worry of what Izzy might get up to among the neighbours' picnic baskets. It had been a very good year for berries, and the community garden at the bottom of the park had yielded plentiful redcurrants earlier in the season. People had seemed reluctant to take the fruit and Jess wondered why that was until a lad approached her and earnestly entreated her not to gather the redcurrants since his mum had warned him that all red berries were poisonous. Jess had replied that while his mother was indeed correct in many instances redcurrants were fine to eat and could be made into crumbles and jellies and summer puddings. The boy had looked blankly at her, she doubted he had ever tasted a summer pudding. He had then run off, only to return shortly with his mother. Pointing at Jess, he begged his mother to instruct her to discard the already picked fruit and step away from the dangerous redcurrants. Jess had thanked the boy for his concern and explained to his mother about redcurrant crumble and jelly. The mother, deeply tanned with streaky blonde hair and wearing a skimpy vest, skinny jeans, high-heeled sandals and heavy-duty sunglasses, said that she hadn't known about redcurrants, but that she relied on the safely advice issued via a parental online forum to avoid all wild red fruit.

"But these are actually cultivated, not wild - try one!" said Jess, offering a spray of redcurrants to the boy. His mother made as if to snatch her son away, almost as though Jess was the wicked queen in a fairy story, tempting the boy with forbidden fruit, but the lad stood his ground and accepted the redcurrants. He tasted them and smiled.

"Try some, Mum, they're nice!"

However, his mother shook her head and grabbing him by the arm, quickly marched her son back the way they had come, preferring to stick with the wisdom of the internet. Jess now noticed the same lad and his mother among one of the barbecue parties, but they had not approached her on this occasion; Jess supposed that the authoritative online parental advice forum might actually sanction blackberries as being safe to eat.

A man she did not recognise strolled over to where Jess was diligently picking. He was shirtless with cut-off denim shorts, and although trying not to stare, Jess could not help noticing that his arms were adorned with a multiplicity of garish tattoos.

"If it's blackberries tha's after love tha' can come and pick in mi garden. I've tons and they're no use to me, they'll only go to waste."

"Thank you," said Jess. "Where do you live?" The man gave an address nearby which Jess recognised as the former home of an acquaintance who had recently moved away. This man must be the new occupant.

The man reached across the bushes extending his hand to Jess.
 "I'm Russ, just moved back to the village after living away for a few years. I'm finding it a bit difficult settling back after all this time."

"And I'm Jess," said Jess, returning the greeting and hoping that Russ would not mind her juice-stained hand. She supposed he would not, since the colour matched many of his tattoos. The man lingered by Jess's blackberry bush as she went on picking so she felt obliged to continue the conversation.

"What took you away from Berringden Brow?" she asked, imagining that the reply would be something along the lines of having left for work reasons, or perhaps because of a relationship.

"Prison, love. Been a resident of HMP 'Ull for seven years."

"Oh dear," said Jess, unable to think of a suitable response. Then curiosity overcame tact. "If you don't mind me asking, what was your offence?"

"Armed robbery, love. Now, don't forget t'blackies, any time will be OK. I don't have to be in, tha'll see them all over t'garden, so just help thissen."

Accordingly, the next evening Jess went round to pick Russ's blackberries. The front garden was a mass of tangled bushes, weighed down with fruit. Beyond the bushes was a wooden cage with a mesh front, containing a small furry creature which Jess recognised as a ferret. As she settled down to her task Russ emerged from the front door, still shirtless but wearing a flat cap. Jess couldn't help wishing that the Indian summer would finally end so that everyone would start putting their clothes back on. Russ was accompanied by a whippet; Jess thought she must have accidentally strayed onto the set of a remake of *Last Of The Summer Wine*. This man was a perfect Yorkshireman cliché. Flat cap, ferret, whippet...

"Just tekking t'dog for a walk; he's not mine, I'm just minding him while mi brother's away. You carry on, love; get as many as tha can."

Jess dared not ask where the brother was, in case he too should turn out to be a guest of Her Majesty. Another neighbour, Bob, came up the street with his dog, Stanley. The two dogs sniffed each other and wagged their tails.

"Eh, Russ lad, don't let Jess get thee talking, tha'll end up in one of her stories," said Bob. He was referring to a collection of locally-set tales which Jess had published some years previously, during Russ's sojourn in Hull. Bob's wife Dot had read Jess's book and now recommended it to all and sundry.

"What's this about stories? I like to read – learned in prison, it helped pass the time. I'll have a copy of this 'ere book of yours Jess. How much is it? Only trouble is, I've no money at the moment, I'm still in the process of sorting everything out."

Jess assured him that he could put the money through her letterbox when his finances were more healthy. She did not enquire what had become of the proceeds of the armed robbery, hoping they had been returned to the rightful owner. She was rather cross with Bob, since she had indeed been thinking of writing a story about Russ, he was after all a significantly more interesting character than the usual array of mundane locals, amongst whom Jess counted herself.

The whippet was by now getting restless so Russ moved off in the direction of the park, while Bob and Stanley headed home leaving Jess alone with the ferret. She completed her fruit picking and returned home to Izzy, just in time to listen to *The Archers*, after which came their evening dog walk. As she led Izzy across the road to the park, Jess realised that the temperature was now much cooler, and heavy clouds were rolling down the valley from the West; it would soon be time for jumpers and cagoules, and thankfully all the skimpy vests and cut-off shorts could be put away for another year.

Chapter 2

At home, Jess was soon busily engaged in washing the berries from Russ's garden in preparation for a jelly-making session, when her friend Nick arrived. Jess and Nick had set up and run an advice centre in a deprived area of the nearby town of Berringden for many years, until the lack of funding obliged it to close; since then Nick had continued with advice work, operating at the end of his mobile phone, without premises, but visiting clients in their own homes. The stream of problems was seemingly never-ending, encompassing welfare benefits, disability rights, debt and immigration. Nick had been living in Jess's attic for a while, ever since a squatter had occupied the house which he had shared with his mother and inherited upon her death, causing him to run away in fright. Jess, with the help of her friend Frank, had eventually managed to evict the squatter, but Nick had been reluctant to return home, explaining that he preferred living in Berringden Brow because it was on a better bus route than his village and also nearer the railway station.

Jess knew that it was not the pleasure of her company which attracted Nick since he stayed out late into the evening visiting clients and was never in any rush to come home to Jess. Nick's house had been left in a damaged state by the squatter and had remained empty until the return of Jess's younger son Alex and his wife Zofia from their world travels, having spent all their money and in need of a home. Jess arranged for the necessary repairs to Nick's house so that Alex and Zofia could move in. They were currently fending off potential squatters who appeared in the garden or were observed peering through the windows from time to time, supposing that the house was still unoccupied. It seemed that word must have got round the local homeless community that there was an empty house, so Alex and Zofia had been obliged to shoo away the uninvited visitors.

Today Nick looked tired as usual, he had worked a lengthy shift seeing more than a dozen people with complicated problems. After patting Izzy, who had greeted him rapturously, he wanted only to rush up to the attic, read the *Racing Post* and listen to the radio. Jess had wondered why he carried on working some years past retirement age but realised that it was his life and that he would still be giving advice if he lived to be ninety. The introduction of Universal Credit had sparked a mass of difficulty for unemployed people, who were often having to wait weeks without any money to live on while their claims were processed. Some were relying on charities such as food banks, or the generosity of relatives, while others fell behind with rent and mortgage payments. Nick was adept at filling in forms and liaising with the benefits department. He frequently represented people at tribunals, usually succeeding in getting clients the benefits which they had been wrongfully denied. His payment was often in kind, a bowl of curry and rice, a bread and butter pudding or a bag of mangoes. With his pension and substantial inheritance, it was not necessary for him to earn a living wage.

Jess was aware that she seemed to have taken over where Nick's mother had left off, acting as landlady and housekeeper. It was not really the retirement she had planned, but she was glad enough to do it for the sake of Alex and Zofia, who were undecided as to what their next move should be and were quite happy living in Nick's house for the time being - despite the infrequency of the buses and lack of proximity to the railway station - since they used their bicycles to get around.

Jess was relieved that she was no longer required to keep up to date with the increasingly complex benefits system. She had begun her career in advice work during the Miners' Strike of 1984 when living in the Selby area. At the time this was part of the Yorkshire coalfield, and the local Citizens Advice Bureau, where Jess had recently completed her volunteer training, had been overwhelmed with enquiries. Apart from giving advice, Jess had collected jumble for the Miners' Wives Support Group and had gone with her friend Hamish to visit a group of women picketing outside Markham Main colliery gate, taking with her a donation of groceries. She and Hamish had had tea with Anne Scargill, wife of the Miners' leader, whom they had bumped into at a rally, and they had also gone to hear Dennis Skinner MP speak in support of the striking miners.

Now, more that thirty years later (and despite the fact that the UK was a prosperous country with the fifth largest economy in the world) many British citizens were still living in hardship and the need for benefits advice had not diminished; while Dennis Skinner, now well into his eighties, had been one of the longest serving Members of Parliament before his eventual retirement. The Selby coalfield, along with others in Yorkshire, had now closed, ending a long tradition of mining in the county.

The evening was growing late and the blackberry juice was left to strain through muslin overnight. A brilliant flash of lightening followed by a loud clap of thunder sent a startled Izzy scuttling upstairs to seek safety, hiding in the bath where it seemed she felt safest. The weather had finally broken.

Chapter 3

The choir of retired people, for which Jess had until recently been the secretary, met every Tuesday lunchtime in the common-room of the local old folks' complex. The group had recently lost their oldest member at the age of 103; happily, Phyllis had enjoyed singing almost until the end of her life. However, such was the demographic make-up of the group that there were inevitably losses through death, illness, removal to live near relatives and banishment to care homes, so that the group rarely numbered more than twenty. Jess had discovered that she was no longer the youngest member of the choir, since a recent addition, a man named Cecil, was three years younger than her, having taken early retirement due to ill health. Cecil not only sang but played the harmonica and the bagpipes. Jess wondered what his neighbours thought about him practicing, but Cecil assured her that they did not mind and in any case his immediate neighbour in the adjoining bungalow was deaf. He had once invited Jess to assist him while busking in Berringden town centre, suggesting that she could pass the hat round after his performance. Jess promptly declined and asked why his girlfriend could not perform this task.

"Oh, Lauren doesn't get out much these days. She's agoraphobic."

"But you said you met her in Tesco so she must go to the shops."

"Well...she does manage to go shopping occasionally. But helping me with the busking would really be far too much for her," said Cecil in his lugubrious tone.

"And also too much for me; I don't care for bagpipes and in any case it's far too chilly now to be standing about for any length of time."

Cecil looked offended, so Jess hoped that he would not ask her again.

Today Cecil informed her that he had recently acquired yet another musical instrument, a melodeon, the only problem being that he did not know how to play it. It so happened that Jess had a friend, Clara, who was an expert on the melodeon and who played for a folk dance group. Clara lived in a village near Selby, close to where Jess had lived many years previously, before her move to Berringden Brow. Jess offered to ask Clara if she would be prepared to give Cecil a tutorial; Jess had actually arranged to visit the Selby area quite soon, since a reading group to which another friend, Lyn, belonged had ordered copies of her book to discuss the following month. She planned to deliver them to Lyn in order to save on the postage, and to have lunch with her. Cecil could have his melodeon lesson with Clara and be collected in the afternoon.

"Do you think Lauren would be up for the trip? A little outing might lift her spirits, and a ride out towards Selby would certainly be more interesting than Tesco's."

"Oh, no, Lauren wouldn't want to listen to me practising the melodeon all morning. And she smokes about forty cigarettes a day, so being at someone else's place would be a problem. Your friend may not want the smell of tobacco in the house and Lauren can't go outside to smoke."

"No, of course not." Jess could imagine Clara's horrified expression if anyone lit up in her house. Jess telephoned Clara, and the trip to

Selby was arranged for the following week, travelling in Jess's car so that she could bring Izzy, rather than leaving her alone at home. However, the evening before they were due to set off Cecil rang Jess, expressing grave concerns as to whether Jess would be able to cope with the traffic on the M62 - after all, so many ladies he knew fought shy of driving on the motorway - so instead he had decided that the safest way would be for him to drive. Jess was extremely annoyed at the idea that she would be intimidated by the motorway - she who had for many years braved the M6 and M5 on the journey to Bristol to visit her elder son Tom when he worked there, and then on to the West Country where her brother still lived; however, she kept her temper and pointed out that she needed to use her own car since she was planning to take Izzy, and in any case was going on to meet Lyn after she had left Cecil and the melodeon at Clara's house. If Cecil had any reservations about her capability as a driver he should take his own car so they could travel in convoy. Cecil hesitated for what seemed to Jess rather an unnecessary length of time.

"No, it's silly to take both cars; all right, we'll go in yours."

By now, Jess was beginning to wish she had never suggested the trip. Her reservations were confirmed immediately she collected Cecil and the melodeon, since he spent the entire twenty-five miles of the journey watching her intently, and passing unhelpful comments regarding what he considered her incorrect use of road lanes, and the fact that in his opinion she had changed up through the gears too quickly. Jess was very relieved to reach Clara's house, and almost pushed Cecil and the melodeon out of the car in her eagerness to see the back of him. Arriving at Lyn's, Jess immediately unburdened herself, complaining how much Cecil's unjustified criticisms had annoyed her, much to the amusement of her friend.

"Where on earth did you find him? What a pain! No wonder his girlfriend doesn't seem to want to go anywhere with him."

"Yes, poor woman, I'd have agoraphobia and smoke forty cigarettes a day if I had to put up with him on a regular basis."

Jess's trials were not yet over for the day, since of course she had to collect Cecil after lunch and return him and the melodeon to his bungalow. She made sure that they set off before the teatime rush hour, but even so, the traffic was building up, so Jess decided that it might be better to leave the motorway and use the A road. Cecil immediately turned to Jess with a stern face.

"Are you sure you know where you're going? We didn't come this way!"

"I'm perfectly sure; I've done this journey dozens of times and anyway I have half a degree in Geography... Look, Cecil, I got you to Clara's on time and I'll get you home in perfect safety."

"OK," dubiously. "Well now, I think we should sort out our next outing."

Jess was so startled that she at once braked and pulled over.

"Whatever do you mean? We aren't having any more outings - this was a one-off, so you could start learning the melodeon!"

"Well, yes, but you suggested it, so it didn't take me long to work out that you must be glad of my company. And you know Jess, you're far too pretty to be on your own..."

Jess could scarcely restrain herself from shoving Cecil onto the grass verge, kidnapping the melodeon and leaving him to find his own way home.

"You've got this completely wrong! Anyway, what about Lauren?"

"Oh; I haven't rung her for a while now, I'm a bit fed up with her, she never wants to go anywhere and besides, kissing her is like kissing an ashtray..."

"Stop!" shouted Jess. "I don't want to go out with you, and anyway I think you should finish with Lauren in a courteous manner, before you start dating any other woman. And you should certainly not criticise her to anyone, she obviously has health problems! Go and see her and explain how you feel."

"Oh, if I did that she would think there was still some hope. It's better just to leave it, she'll realise in time when I don't phone."

"Well, I think it's always much better to be clear about these things." Jess, having recovered her composure a little, set off again, aware that it would soon be Izzy's teatime. Luckily, the little dog was still asleep on the back seat.

"We can at least go for a walk together surely," said Cecil as the car drew up outside his house. Jess kept the engine running.

"We won't be going for a walk or anything else! I don't want to!"

"Really Jess, I simply cannot understand why any woman would prefer to be on her own when there's a man available," mused Cecil, reaching for his melodeon. "Now, how about coming in for a cup of tea and maybe a quick listen to me playing the bagpipes?"

"Cecil; **No!**"

Jess roared off with such speed that Izzy woke up, startled. However, by the time they reached home, Jess was beginning to see the funny side of the day's events. She fed Izzy, then phoned Lyn to let her know she had arrived home safely and to bring her up to date on the Cecil story, and soon they were both laughing at his obtuseness and antediluvian views on women. They agreed that the unfortunate Lauren was well rid of him. Really, it was scarcely possible to believe that men like him still existed; his attitudes to women were distinctly unpleasant - Victorian even, decided Jess, remembering her own father, born at the turn of the twentieth century, and his decree that a woman's role was to serve men and that education was therefore wasted on a girl. (His refusal to complete the required grant

15

application forms in order for Jess to take up her university place had caused all sorts of problems, necessitating the involvement of the Grammar School Headmaster and an appeal to Devon County Hall for Jess's mother to be allowed to fill out the forms, back in the days when widows were the only women permitted to conduct their own affairs and a married women's income was deemed to belong to her husband.) Evidently the feminist revolution and gaining of hard-won rights by women during the intervening half-century had been completely ignored by men such as Cecil. Jess resolved to give choir a miss for a few weeks as she reached for her phone in order to block Cecil's number.

Chapter 4

Jess answered the phone one morning to her younger son, Alex, who had been away all summer stewarding at music festivals around the country. His wife of almost a year, Zofia, whom he had married in Las Vegas the previous November, was working in a café near Berringden Brow, and Alex had been coming home in between festivals to see her.

"Hi Mum, hope you are OK? Now, don't get alarmed, but I'm in hospital in Kidderminster..." here he broke off as a voice called loudly in the distance, 'Kettering! You're in Kettering Hospital!'
"Oh, I'm in Kettering apparently. I knew it was somewhere in the Midlands beginning with K. Anyway, I've broken my leg, tripped over a tree stump in the dark last night. I've arranged for Kelly to collect me in her van where there'll be room to keep my leg up, she's coming with Zofia later on today to take me back to Yorkshire so I can be transferred to Huddersfield; they don't do orthopaedics in Berringden any more and I don't want to be stuck here, so far away from Zofia and you and all my mates. So I'll text once I'm there and you can visit me tomorrow if you want."

Jess was shocked and had a number of questions but Alex interrupted her, "Sorry Mum, the doctor's on his rounds, can't keep him waiting." Jess spent an anxious day waiting for further news. Alex duly arrived in Huddersfield and was admitted to the Royal Infirmary during the evening, his X-rays having been emailed through from Kettering.

"It's such a relief to be back in Yorkshire, the nurses are much more friendly here, that ward sister in Kettering was a right battle-axe. My leg hurts like hell, they can't operate until the swelling goes down and they can't say how long that will take. I'm in a private room on a cancer ward, the orthopaedic ward was full. I'm just glad they could find somewhere to put me. I'm waiting for them to bring me more pain-killers. The doctor asked all about my drinking habits and he nearly hit the roof when I told him how much I drank. Bet he's never been to a festival, what does he expect, drinking goes with the territory. I'll see you tomorrow. Got to go, the painkillers are here."

Jess put down the phone with mixed feelings. Naturally she was sorry that Alex had broken his leg and was in pain, but relieved that he had made it safely back to Yorkshire. As for his drinking, Jess reflected that at least while he was in hospital he would have to stop, so that his body would have a rest from the unremitting onslaught of alcohol. Maybe this broken leg would turn out to be an unlikely blessing in disguise. Jess remembered her own father, continually inebriated throughout the 1960s, and the terrible emotional damage his drunken rages had inflicted upon his fearful family. She sometimes wondered if she had inadvertently passed on the drinking habit to Alex through a faulty gene which had not manifested itself in her own case; but even if that was the case, there was nothing she could do about it, only try to support Alex as best she could.

Jess drove Zofia to Huddersfield the next day where they found Alex with his foot raised, alone in his side room with no-one to talk to.

"The TV doesn't work so I'm bored as hell!. What did you bring - grapes? How traditional. Something to read? I've already read that one! At least I've got plenty of music on my phone..."

Fortunately, the swelling went down after a few days so Alex could have the operation to reset the broken bone. To Jess's astonishment, he was discharged the following day. She supposed that they needed the bed, and at least there would be more to amuse Alex at home. Once he was safely installed on the sofa with plenty of cushions for support, Jess went to see him. She found him in good spirits, drinking a turmeric shake which Zofia had concocted.

"Turmeric's very healing, very anti-inflammatory. I'm so glad to be home, Mum. Guess what, I didn't get the dreaded Delirium tremens, despite what the doctor thought."

"It'll have done you good, being obliged to lay off the drink for a week or so. Don't rush back to the bottle - allow your body time to heal. Alex, I'll say this to your face, you are a much nicer person when you're sober. Too much drink tends to make people nasty, just like my father was nasty when he'd had too much, which was most of the time. That's why my mother had to sleep in my bedroom, with our door barricaded with a chest of drawers. You don't want to get into that state, driving away all your family and friends."

"Mum, I know I should take better care of myself and I will from now on. But don't nag me; I know what to do to get myself better, and nagging won't help. So we'll say no more about it. Where's the cat? He's been lying beside me, he's really a great comfort. Animals can sense all kinds of things - they pick up on our emotions when people can be blind to them. And stroking animals helps a lot, with blood pressure and calmness. Can you ask Zofia to find Nev for me please; he's hiding somewhere, he probably thinks you've brought Izzy, and of course they don't get on. He'll most likely emerge when you've gone. He's all the therapy I need at the moment."

Jess decided to sit up late that evening after her bath to watch a film about Cary Grant, recalling the long-ago days when she and her brother Jeff had been at school with Barbara Harris, who had gone on to become the celebrated actor's fifth wife. Much later, Jess's son Tom had been at university in Bristol and had for a time lived in Picton Street, which had been Grant's home when he was known by his original name, Archie Leach. However, Jess's enjoyment of the film was ruined by the loud noise coming from her new next-door neighbour's house. This had recently been rented by a young woman with two small children, so Jess had called round to welcome her to the neighbourhood and explain which day the bins were emptied and where it was necessary to retrieve them from afterwards, since the bin-men never returned them, but left them at the end of the street. The woman had said her name was Abby and that she had come from Keighley, but did not seem to want to say anything more, and Jess had concluded that she was the sort of person who might wish to keep herself to herself. Jess often heard the children screaming through the thin party wall, and there was sometimes a great deal of hammering, but tonight, Jess could hear a man's voice, using simply appalling language. The ranting and raving went on for about twenty minutes so that Jess found it necessary to turn up the volume on her TV in order to catch the dialogue. Next she was obliged to switch on the sub-titles. Then she began to worry about the safety of the young woman and children, although there was no sound from them. Was the man shouting at Abby, or maybe into his phone? Jess was unsure what action to take. She recalled lurid press reports of murders where abused women had been killed by violent partners or ex-partners, and everyone asked "But where were the neighbours when all this was going on?" On the other hand, whatever was happening next door was clearly none of her business and moreover she did not want to put herself in danger.

Eventually, Jess could stand it no longer, so she wrapped her dressing gown tightly around herself and knocked on the neighbour's door. It opened to reveal a tall, dark, curly-haired, youngish man, who looked at her enquiringly.

"You're probably unaware, but the partition wall between these houses is very thin and I can clearly hear *every word* you are saying," said Jess, fully expecting a reply along the lines of, "Shove off, it's nothing at all to do with you!"

To her surprise the man apologised politely, saying he would keep the noise down. There was no sign of anyone else, and Jess reckoned that if the young woman had been in any kind of danger she could have taken the opportunity to ask for Jess's help. She therefore concluded that the man must have been having a fierce argument with someone on the phone. Jess returned to her own house, where the Cary Grant film was still playing on the TV, but by now Jess had completely lost the thread and decided to go to bed.

Chapter 5

It was time for the annual visit of Jess's old friend Edwin. He came up from the Kent coast and usually stayed for four days, but this year had announced that he could only stay for two nights because his girlfriend needed him to take her back home after a hen weekend near York. The girlfriend, Emel, was a recent addition to Edwin's life, she was considerably younger than septuagenarian Edwin and Jess was intrigued as to how they had met. Edwin told her that Emel had originally been his hairdresser before being promoted to her new status. She was due to attend the women-only weekend at a luxury spa hotel, which was how Edwin came to be free for these particular two days. He would bring Emel to York, deliver her to the hotel, then travel to see Jess in the Pennines before escorting Emel back home.

Jess tidied up her spare bedroom and put fresh bedding on the divan. Edwin seemed rather disconcerted when she showed him into the smaller attic room.

"Don't I usually have the larger attic?"

"Nick's in there now, so this is the only spare room I have."

"Hm; are you sure this room has been thoroughly aired, Jess?"

Jess tried to conceal her annoyance "Of course, I had the window open until the rain started, then I closed it. Why don't you unpack, then come down and we can have a cup of tea?"

"Ah, tea; I don't suppose you have any oat or almond milk, do you? If not I'll have to go to the shop, as I don't drink cow's milk now."

Jess was surprised to hear this since Edwin had hitherto been a great fan of dairy products, especially ice-cream. Edwin noted her expression and explained that milk and cream were the only dairy items he had given up, as the further the product was from the cow the less it seemed to affect him, so it was still fine for him to consume the long-standing favourites, cheese and ice-cream.

Jess had been planning to make Eton Mess for dessert but Edwin said that nowadays he would prefer yoghurt to cream. Jess had none in the fridge, nor did she keep an alternative range of milks in the house, but luckily the village convenience store now stocked some of these products, so Jess collected Izzy's lead and they all walked down the the shop. Edwin also needed to pick up a paper, he bought the *Guardian* every day and spent each evening snipping out pieces of interest, to be filed away in plastic carrier bags. He always brought his own scissors with him especially for snipping purposes. Jess had pointed out that national newspapers carried extensive online archives nowadays, rendering all the laborious cutting out quite unnecessary; but Edwin insisted he still preferred hard copy.

"Do you ever actually refer to any of the articles you've saved?" asked Jess. Edwin admitted that he did not, he simply stored the pieces in their plastic bags. However, Jess supposed that cutting up the paper was a harmless enough occupation and anyway was firmly entrenched in Edwin's routine.

"What does Emel think of your evenings' snipping? Wouldn't she prefer you to be watching a film with her perhaps?"

Edwin looked sheepish. "Emel doesn't know about me cutting up the papers, I never do it when I'm with her as she likes everything very tidy, so I have to save up all the papers until I'm back home, or with someone like you who doesn't mind..."

Jess had found the paper snipping quite irritating at first, since she always discovered lots of tiny pieces of paper under the sofa or behind the cushions after Edwin left; but she had become resigned to it after so many years.

"What does Emel like to do?" asked Jess, sipping her tea.

"Oh, well; I suppose her favourite hobby is shopping. She likes to go into Marks and Spencer and try on tops – in fact that's what we did this morning after we arrived in York. She's really not much of a one for sight-seeing..."

"What about books?" asked Jess, knowing that Edwin was a great reader and collector, with all the rooms in his house plus a large garden shed devoted to floor to ceiling book storage.

"Oh, goodness, no: she leafs through magazines but doesn't really read. And she likes to flick through the TV channels when we stay in hotels."

Edwin confessed that Emel was not very complimentary about his choice of hotels for their rendezvous, they generally stayed in a travel lodge, so he had let her pick the accommodation for their forthcoming holiday in Malta. They were planning to stay at the Holiday Inn, near a shopping centre, although Edwin hoped to be able to get away at some point to view the Roman ruins. Jess marvelled that a neatness-loving shopaholic had managed to capture the heart of a man whose interests were books, sight-seeing at ancient monuments and daily newspaper snipping. She reflected that love is indeed very strange.

The following day Jess proposed a visit to Shibden Hall, where visitor numbers had recently experienced a huge increase following the screening of the Sunday evening television series, "Gentleman Jack" based on the life of local nineteenth century landowner, Anne Lister. Jess recalled the sensation when extracts from Anne's decoded diaries were published in the 1980s, revealing a succession of lesbian affairs. As well as rooms furnished in the manner of Anne Lister's day, Shibden also had a folk museum which boasted the country's oldest preserved carriage, although Jess thought it looked to be badly in need of further preservation measures. Edwin found the visit interesting, but after a couple of hours both he and Jess felt in need of a cup of tea. Jess asked one of the Hall's stewards what had become of the teashop she remembered from a previous visit, and was told that it was currently closed and that the nearest café could be found at the bottom of the park, by the lake. Edwin and Jess accordingly made their way through the park, where the café was very busy and the queue extremely long. When she reached the front of the queue Jess ordered two bowls of soup, thinking it could simply be ladled out, but was told that there would be a half-hour wait for all hot food, even soup, so they were obliged to order tea and packets of crisps, the only food immediately available at the counter. They took their snack to an outside table, no indoor ones being available.

"Not much of a lunch," sighed Jess. Edwin was becoming cross because his paper napkin was blowing away across the grass.

"I hate eating out of doors," grumbled Edwin, retrieving the napkin and ramming it under the milk-jug. Jess offered to look to see if an indoor table had become free. Edwin glumly shook his head and began munching his crisps.

"They don't seem to have been able to keep up with all the extra visitors. Maybe they should consider taking on more staff at weekends," said Jess, hoping that the drop of moisture she had just felt on her face was not the beginning of a shower, since it would be no fun sitting outside in the rain. They ate their meagre lunch, Jess thinking about Anne Lister and her brave resistance to the local domineering male mine owners who had tried to steal coal from the Shibden pits, while Edwin debated whether or not to buy an ice-cream. He had noticed a stall selling a brand he particularly liked with an array of tempting flavours. Jess knew that any expedition with Edwin invariable involved eating at least one ice-cream, no matter how chilly the weather, and today was no exception.

Luckily they managed to finish their lunch and make their way back to the car before the weather worsened. Jess said that she ought to go home to see about Izzy's afternoon walk so she left Edwin at the Industrial Museum for an hour of historical sight-seeing based on Berringden's history of toffee-making, moquette-weaving, engineering, coal-mining and the manufacture of cats' eyes. At least I don't make him wait for ages outside the changing rooms in clothes stores, reflected Jess, recalling Edwin's account of his shopping trips with Emel. She hoped she had at least given Edwin a welcome opportunity to do something other than visit M and S. Izzy was as always delighted to see Jess, and Jess was relieved to have a short respite from her duties as tour guide and hostess. The rain was easing as she and Izzy left the house and crossed the park, and Jess was pleased to notice a rainbow forming over the valley.

Edwin returned on the tea-time train, full of praise for the efforts of the volunteers who staffed the Industrial Museum. Jess suggested a trip to the local pub; however, her guest pointed out that he was still way behind with his paper snipping, and it being Saturday, he always bought two quality papers, so there was double the work to contend with. Jess had hoped they could get some food at the pub, but resigned herself to cooking. She had some vegetables in the fridge so decided to use them up in a ratatouille, to be eaten with baked potatoes, usually a safe bet for someone who does not eat meat. Edwin thanked her for an interesting day and delicious meal, then ensconced himself on the sofa with his newspapers and scissors. He broke off from his assiduous snipping to read a text from Emel, informing him that the spa weekend was going well; it had begun with a pyjama party and there was a character present called The Butler looking after the women and giving them instructions on how to play various 'hen games'. This all sounded rather strange to Jess, who had never been on a spa weekend and did not know quite what one might expect on such occasions. She had imagined relaxing massages and saunas rather than pyjama parties and games with a butler. The things some middle-aged women got up to these days... Then Jess thought back to local heroine Anne Lister and how she had valiantly disregarded many of the social conventions of the early nineteenth century. Bold women had always pushed the boundaries, including the twentieth century suffragettes and the campaigners for women's equal rights in the 1970s, and Jess felt that their efforts should be applauded, not disparaged; and if modern women wanted to spend a racy spa weekend away from their menfolk then there was absolutely no harm in that.

Chapter 6

Jess's former Barn Dance partner, Frank, was on the phone, coughing and sneezing and complaining that his cat had fleas yet again. Jess advised him to thoroughly hoover the house from top to bottom. Frank replied weakly that his vacuum cleaner had broken down six weeks ago so he was unable to do any cleaning. He had replaced the fuse but the machine still would not work, he had no idea what was wrong... However, even at thirty miles distance, Jess had a good idea as to what might be the matter. For many years Frank had not cut his hair, which was by now waist length and worn in a straggly grey pony tail. Frank and the cat both shed hairs everywhere, and Jess suspected these might have clogged up the vacuum cleaner. She suggested that Frank should immediately investigate but he replied that any attempt at this would certainly trigger his allergies.

"Wear a face mask! You say the vacuum cleaner stopped working six weeks ago so the house must be inches under dust! Get someone to have a look at it, or take it to a repair shop, or buy a new one if all else fails!"

As usual, Frank had a long list of excuses as to why he could not follow any of Jess's suggestions. There were no repair men in the village where he lived, he could not afford the call-out charge for anyone to come and look at it, and he certainly could not afford to buy a new one, nor even second-hand...

After a previous call from a man in need of Jess's help, her cousin Jan, on a visit from Canada some years ago, had asked in a puzzled voice whether Jess didn't have any nice girlfriends. Jess replied that she had several, but they were all sensible women, married and settled and frequently occupied running local organisations and caring for their grandchildren. Jess met up with Lyn and other members of their former baby-sitting group a couple of times a year, but finding a date to suit all of these busy women was difficult. Similarly, the group with whom Jess had been at university all led busy lives and one was now lecturing overseas, so getting everyone together was almost impossible and could only take place when Professor Jane happened to be in the UK for an academic conference. Jess had explained to her cousin that it always seemed to be men who turned to her for support, while her female friends were either well able to look after themselves, or had helpful husbands.

Jess and Nick had been obliged to travel the thirty miles to Frank's village in order to clear his garden the previous summer, since he had been under orders from the local Environmental Health department to dispose of a quantity of rotting timber, consisting of a collapsed shed and a collection of decaying fence panels, believed to be harbouring rodents. The task must be completed within a fortnight to avoid legal action and the enforcement officer would visit to check the situation two weeks from the date on which the notice had been served. Frank had declared himself much too unwell to tackle the job, nor could he find anyone locally to do the work, although Jess wondered if he had tried very hard, if at all. Frank complained bitterly about the injustice of the situation and how he was being victimised by the local authority. Wishing to spare Frank a summons, a fine, or possible imprisonment if the fine was not paid - and also keen to spare herself any more of Frank's dismal phone calls - Jess had enlisted Nick's help in clearing the garden; it had taken the entire weekend and many trips to the tip during a heatwave, but their efforts had saved the day. Now it seemed that they would to have to sacrifice yet another weekend cleaning Frank's house in order to protect his variable health. He had a multiplicity of allergies and ailments, but Jess knew it would be futile to suggest hiring a cleaner, since he would refuse point blank.

Jess's son Tom, phoning from London, having recently moved from

Bristol, expressed surprise and a degree of exasperation on hearing that she was yet again about to set off on a mercy mission to Frank's.

"I thought you were giving up all this dashing round the countryside, wearing yourself out. You agreed with me that you should look after yourself and enjoy life rather than indulging this strange compulsion to help people who are perfectly capable of doing things for themselves but prefer to rely on you instead! Anyway, weren't you over there recently, fitting a carpet or something?"

Jess and Nick had indeed spent a day removing the worn out holey rag on Frank's stairs, which Jess considered a danger to life and limb and about which she had been warning Frank for years, and replacing it with the decent mid-blue carpet from Jess's spare room. An emigrating friend had passed on a good piece of Axminster which would do for the spare room, so the blue carpet had become surplus to requirements. Frank had actually caught his foot in the old stair carpet and tripped; he had not confessed to Jess about this incident, but she had heard about it from their mutual friend Clara, so the new carpet had arrived not a moment too soon, before further accidents.

"The thing is, Tom, that when someone is living with depression they often can't face tackling even the simplest of tasks without help. We're just trying to improve Frank's life in a small way so that he might perhaps feel a bit better. And he has helped me in the past, looking after Izzy while we were away, and he came with me to evict Nick's squatter when I needed support and you were in Bristol."

"Well, I applaud your altruism, but please don't overdo it, Mum. You're well into your sixties now, remember. I don't want to be visiting you in hospital after you've worn yourself out helping all and sundry."

Jess appreciated Tom's concern but felt that she might be equal to the task of repairing a hair-clogged hoover. Nick assembled various tools which might be required and they set off.

Jess glanced around Frank's kitchen, looking for the vacuum cleaner.

"It's here!" said Frank, removing an assortment of coats hanging over the handle and completely disguising the machine. Jess examined it, and as she had suspected, the head was choked with long grey hairs, wrapped in a thick clump around the brushes. Jess seized a pair of scissors from the kitchen drawer and began cutting away the hair. "You could have made a start with this," she grumbled.

"Don't use those! They're the best scissors; use the old ones!" exclaimed Frank in an annoyed tone. "Anyway, I've been far too busy recently to attend to it. I've had a number of extremely complicated country dance sequences to work on."

Frank taught country dancing at a U3A group, a duty he took very seriously. He and his next door neighbours were engaged in a musical war, with the neighbours blasting deafening pop numbers through the party wall while Frank retaliated with equally loud square dance music. Jess was by now well into her task and determined not to relinquish the sharp scissors. Izzy was rolling in the hayfield which constituted Frank's un-mown front lawn, while Frank's cat had retreated to the safety of the coal bunker roof and was eyeing Izzy with alarm. Meanwhile Nick was arranging his assortment of screwdrivers and spanners.

"I'll check the fuse by swapping the one from the kettle into the hoover, since at least we know that one works."

Between them, Jess and Nick managed to get the hoover working within ten minutes of arriving. Nick emptied the dirt from the brimming hoover barrel, Jess replaced the kettle fuse, and they all sat down for a cup of tea. The dust everywhere was badly affecting Jess and Nick, and even Izzy was now sneezing. Frank of course was perpetually coughing and spluttering. Jess was annoyed to discover that the recently-fitted blue stair carpet was now swathed in dusty long grey hairs, like the rest of the house. Frank did not appear to have made any attempt to keep it clean.

"Well, I couldn't hoover it, could I?" said Frank, defensively.

"But you could have used a dustpan and brush!" said Jess.

Frank made a weak excuse about the blue carpet being very difficult to clean and his brush not having strong enough bristles, adding plaintively, "And now I'm being bullied!"

"Well, I always managed to clean the blue carpet when it was in my spare room with no difficulty whatsoever!"

Jess seized the bush and soon had the stair carpet blue again. She also swept the Artex wall covering on the staircase, which was festooned with dust and cobwebs. Then she had another sneezing fit. Jess wished that the TV programme *How Clean Is Your House?* was still being broadcast, so that she could have sent Kim Woodburn and Aggie Mackenzie and their crack cleaning team round to Frank's house; they would soon have had it sparkling. Jess noted that the forlorn plant on the landing windowsill had died, it appeared to have succumbed to the dust stifling every leaf pore. She remembered the celebrity Quentin Crisp remarking during a television interview that in his experience a dust layer did not get noticeably worse after four years; Jess wondered if maybe Frank was trying to replicate this testimony; but perhaps Quentin Crisp had not had any house plants at risk of suffocation. Jess threw open the grimy landing window - apparently no window cleaner had visited the house for many years - aware that the sun had now come out. The house could do with a good airing; and it was time to take Izzy for a walk so that they could all get some much-needed fresh air.

Chapter 7

Jess's brother Jeff rang from the West Country, requesting her exact date of birth, address and postcode, which were required for an application form he was completing. Jeff had been invited to apply for a position on a scrutiny panel assisting the elected Police Commissioner for Devon and Cornwall force; the form was several pages long and required information about all the candidate's siblings. It also asked for details of membership of political parties and campaign groups.

"Goodness, what on earth for? You are a man of probity who has been involved with voluntary organisations for decades and can provide excellent references - so what if your radical sister belonged to the Campaign for Nuclear Disarmament or the League against Cruel Sports? The fact that I camped at Greenham Common in the early 80s, and went to the Stop Trident rally in Barrow-in-Furness in 1984 and on the 2003 Stop The War march should not affect your chances! Are you sure you want to include me on the form? Although currently the only groups I belong to are the Dogs Trust and the Women's Institute and they could scarcely object to those..."

"I don't know how thoroughly they will check. It's not as though you have a criminal record or anything like that. But if I failed to disclose you maybe they have a way of tracing you through official records and I'd be shown up as having something to hide. I'm actually quite surprised they want all this information since I thought they already knew everything about us. I'm sure they have facial recognition software to identify everyone who goes on those marches. Maybe it's a test of my honesty, to see if I admit to you being my sister when they are already aware of you, so I'll put you down just in case."

"Jeff, have you never taken part in any sort of protest? I seem to recall you were in the campaign to allow home-knitted jumpers at school, when the Headmaster was insisting we must all buy those expensive ones from the authorised stockist. Didn't that make the local news?"
"I doubt they'll cast their net as far back as the provincial news of 1968. And the only protest march I went on was when Mrs. Thatcher snatched the school milk."

"Well, it will be interesting to see how far you get with the application. Let me know if you are called for interview, and maybe you'd better be prepared to answer a question about how you came to be a pillar of society when your sister with the same family background turned out to be such a radical..."

Jess thought back to the years of her campaigning and demonstrating which had begun in the 1980s in Selby, when she had answered a request in the local paper for people to join the newly-resurrected local branch of the Campaign for Nuclear Disarmament. The Selby Times piece had given a man named Hamish as a contact, so Jess had phoned and joined up. As a single parent, she was deeply concerned about the future of a world with Cruise missiles. Jess had gone with Hamish and the rest of the local group on a number of marches, and she had also camped for a weekend at Greenham Common, where the Cruise missiles were sited. The women living there permanently had declared an open weekend, and people from all over the country were rallying around the base perimeter. Jess and two women friends had taken a tent, but there were no sanitary facilities available so Jess had insisted that they find a place with plenty of trees and shrubs. She and one of her companions had been pregnant at the time, with resulting bladder pressure problems. The three friends had chosen a shady spot near Orange gate, and later joined the encirclement of the base with everyone holding hands and singing songs. It had been a very memorable experience. The missiles had eventually been removed, but on revisiting the area with her sons some years later Jess had found that there was still a small peace camp, since there were a number of on-going wars around the world, notably the illegal conflict in Iraq. Jess told Alex that he had actually been to Greenham while still in her belly. There were very few men at the weekend event she had attended, apart from local tradesmen mending the fence, so Alex had been part of a select minority, although he seemed quite unimpressed with this revelation.

At the time of Jess original Greenham visit six-year-old Tom had been spending the weekend with his father Bill, whose favourite occupation during the autumn was walking over newly-ploughed fields with a metal detector, searching for buried treasure. Occasionally he found a pre-decimal coin, and once he had unearthed an ancient brooch which he donated to the local museum, but the expeditions were mostly fruitless. However, they provided fresh air and exercise. Jess hoped that Tom understood why his parents had been unable to live together, since they had very different interests and outlook, although they were still friends.

By coincidence, Hamish, now living in Doncaster, rang Jess that evening, jubilantly explaining that he had finally got to grips with the sophisticated mobile phone his son had given him for his birthday.

"Ian said I have to go into contacts, but I didn't understand how to get you into the contact list in the first place. Luckily Ian came at the weekend and showed me what to do. He's put you in at the top of the list, Jess darling, you're my oldest friend. Anyway, the reason I rang was to find out when we are next meeting up."

Jess remembered that Nick was planning to go over to Doncaster for the races the Saturday after next so she arranged to meet Hamish after dropping Nick at the racecourse. Their meetings these days usually took the form of a gentle stroll and a pub meal, rather than the rigours of political marches or demonstrations, as octogenarian Hamish's health had deteriorated after a recent bout of illness.

"We could look around that Wildlife Park, if you are up for it. It was on the local news recently, they've rescued some lions from a grubby Romanian zoo."

"Och that would be great. They might have a wheelchair I can borrow if I get tired. You know, the animal I've always wanted to see is a giraffe, I'd like to go up on one of those platforms, so you can look them in the eye and feed leaves to them. I'll look forward to it!"

It so happened that Alex had borrowed a wheelchair when his broken leg required support; he had rigged up a board at the front on which to stretch out the injured limb, but his leg was healing so well that he no longer required the wheelchair, and Jess resolved to put it in the boot of the car for Hamish to use if required.

Chapter 8

Jess and Nick set off for Doncaster, leaving Izzy with dog-loving neighbours Pam and Sam. Nick got out at the racecourse, and Jess went to collect Hamish, who announced that he was having a good day, so would not require the wheelchair. Jess assured him that they would in any case take things at a gentle pace. There were plenty of cafés and other places to sit down as they made their leisurely way around the park. It was a warm day, and Jess felt sorry for the Polar Bears, enduring the Tropic of Doncaster. However, they had a large lake in which to take refreshing dips. One bear seemed intent on chasing a duck which had had the temerity to swim in the bears' lake, but the duck was apparently well aware of the danger and managed to stay ahead of its ursine pursuer. Having next made a point of visiting the giraffes, they stopped for a rest beside the monkey enclosure and ate ice-creams.

"See how that little one is clinging on to its mother! So small yet it knows just what it has to do to stay alive. Nature's just amazing!"

Jess agreed, but added that she was not very fond of monkeys.

"When we were in Zimbabwe the vervet monkeys would jump down from the trees and pinch the sugar packets from the cafés, then rush back up into the branches, rip the packets open, and shower everyone underneath with sugar! Then the baboons would break through the camp-site fence, bold as brass, undo the tent zips, take stuff such as jam-jars and open them, eat the contents and throw the jars down. You either had to take your food with you when you went out each day or suspend it in bags from tree branches which the baboons were too heavy to walk along and which they couldn't reach from the ground. Whoever invents a baboon-proof tent will make a fortune."

"But those are sensible strategies as far as the monkeys are concerned, if humans leave easily obtainable food lying around they're bound to take it. I'd forgotten that you had been in Africa, Jess; I suppose that was the one good thing that came about from your time with Robin, wasn't it, the opportunity to visit him there."

"Yes, I would never have gone if it hadn't been for him. It was a wonderful opportunity for Alex, too. But I'm glad I didn't stay, even though I was offered a job there. Robin had found a new partner, I would have been homesick and Tom was at Bristol uni then, so I would have been thousands of miles away from him. Then there was the AIDS crisis, several of our friends died with it, both Europeans and Africans. They have better drugs to treat it now but there was nothing very effective at the time."

"Well, maybe it's time we made our way back to town. I'm starting to feel rather tired," said Hamish, reaching for his walking stick.

"Yes of course; and Nick will be leaving the races soon. I hope he's had a successful afternoon and won lots of money. He has some sort of system but he never lets on, and you wouldn't think it from his appearance; he's hardly a snazzy dresser - he wears his clothes and shoes until they literally go into holes and I end up throwing them out which makes him cross since he's then obliged to buy new ones."

"Nick's never really been one to splash the cash, has he... although he does take you on those cruises, which is very generous of him."

"Yes, I shouldn't complain. Of course they are sold as 'two-for-one' if you book early enough - BOGOF cruises - so I actually go free."

"Maybe I should consider going on a cruise now my hiking days are over." mused Hamish. " I might meet a rich widow, although of course we men are programmed to always desire still-fertile women, so she wouldn't have to be too old..."

"Or you might simply have a relaxing time, seeing new places and meeting interesting people, " said Jess, deciding not to rise to the challenge of arguing with Hamish about his oft-repeated assertion regarding the alleged lack of unattractiveness of older women, as arm in arm they headed towards the exit.

Chapter 9

Jess was on her way to London to attend a lesson at the cookery school owned by celebrity chef Ariadne Wick. Jess had very little interest in cooking and had not really wanted to go, but her friend Martha had insisted. Martha's husband took part in every *Daily Mail* competition, whether he actually wanted the prize or not. He had won the cookery lesson, but did not wish to take it up, and Martha was unable to go to London on that particular day so had talked Jess into accepting the prize. Jess had tried her best to refuse, suggesting that Martha must know someone far more interested in cookery than she was who could make better use of the 'Healthy Cooking' lesson. However, Martha seemed quite determined that Jess should go.

"You can use the opportunity to visit Tom at the same time. No-one else we know has a relative in London they could stay with so of course I thought of you. Maybe you can pass on the recipes when you get back."

The cookery lesson was scheduled to start quite early in the morning, so it was necessary for Jess to travel to London the previous day. Her train got into Kings Cross just after lunch and she was met by Tom who had taken the afternoon off work to meet her. He suggested that they might go round the corner to the exhibition of Anglo-Saxon treasures at the British Library. Jess was always happy to visit the British Library, since she had been required to supply a free copy of her own little book under the legal deposit scheme, which applied to every publication in the UK. She knew that a copy of her book must be stored somewhere within the precincts, although she understood that there could not be enough room in the main library to shelve every publication; she imagined there must be vast underground stacks housing the works of lesser-known writers such as herself. Today, Jess and Tom saw the wonderful Anglo-Saxon illuminated manuscripts and various priceless artefacts, some unearthed by the use of metal detectors; they agreed that life-long metal detectorist, Bill, would have appreciated the exhibition. He had discovered many curios over the years but was yet to find a significant hoard.

After a pub meal Jess and Tom made their way back to Tom's house where Jess set her alarm for early the next morning, since she would have to cross London during the height of the rush hour, along with all the thousands of people going to work. Tom escorted Jess to the local station and saw her onto a commuter train. It was very crowded and Jess was the last passenger to board at that particular stop, so that Tom had to give his mother a shove in order to get her up the step and into the packed carriage. The journey to the cookery school involved several changes, the final leg being by bus, followed by a short walk. The school had provided instructions as to where to alight from the bus, but Jess could see no sign of the school itself. She was at the intersection of five roads, none of which appeared to be the street she was looking for. She spotted a policeman on the opposite pavement and asked him where the Ariadne Wick cookery school might be. He shook his head and said he had never heard of it.

Jess was then reduced to running up and down asking passers-by if they had any idea of the whereabouts of the cookery school; she felt rather like Anneka Rice must have done in the old *Treasure Hunt* programmes, except of course that Jess was not fetchingly attired in a flying suit but was sporting her dull blue padded jacket. Several people resorted to looking at maps on their phones, but this did not seem to help since nobody appeared to really understand them. One person told Jess that the school was five minutes up a particular road but as she set off he called her back saying that it looked as though one of the other streets was actually quicker at only three minutes. Eventually, after lots of blank looks and shaking of heads and remarks in languages which Jess did not understand she found someone who could accurately direct her to the cookery school, still several streets away. Jess raced through the door, thoroughly dishevelled after her arduous commute and stressful search, arriving just as the lesson was about to start. The instructor, naturally not Ariadne herself, kindly allowed the scarlet-faced and breathless Jess to have a few minutes in which to swallow a drink of water and go to the loo before the lesson commenced.

There then began a hectic morning of non-stop cooking, such as Jess had not experienced since her O level cookery practical exam fifty years previously. On that baking summer day the school Domestic Science room had been sweltering, with ovens and hobs going at full blast as a dozen girls prepared their exam meal, with the sun beating relentlessly through the windows. Jess had almost fainted with the heat and anxiety, she wondered how her fellow cooks were so calm, cool and collected as they went about their various tasks. At least the cookery teacher's two dogs had been banished for the day, so that there was no risk of tripping over a cocker spaniel, generally an occupational hazard in the Domestic Science room. Jess's work station was nearest the door, so that during cookery lessons she was often required to respond to a imperious instruction from the teacher to down tools in order to let one or other of the dogs out to relieve itself on the hockey pitch and then to let the animal back in when it returned and scratched at the door. Thankfully, today that was one worry she need not have.

Jess's assignment, allocated the previous week, had been to prepare a picnic for two archaeological students going on a dig, to include a cooked dish, a sweet and a freshly prepared drink. She was also required to provide a quick and easy supper dish for their return. Jess was making meatloaf, salad, shortbread biscuits and home-made lemonade, with a creation of mashed potato nests of tinned tomatoes and poached eggs for supper. In reality the archaeological students would surely have packed sandwiches, crisps and pop, and opened a tin of beans for their evening meal. Jess had run into some difficulty when the potato nests would not brown sufficiently nor the eggs properly poach in the tomato juice despite the oven being turned up very high. The examiner had noticed her distress and kindly suggested that she pop it all under the grill to quickly brown, which had worked perfectly. Jess had passed the exam at Grade 2, in the days when Grade 1 was high and nine a fail, unlike modern times where the scale has been inverted. She felt very pleased with herself but had never again attempted to make either meat loaf or the poached egg, tomato and potato supper dish.

Today there were ten cooks present – nine women and one man –

who were all required to complete a lengthy list of dishes before they could sit down to a late lunch. Jess's lack of chopping ability was noted, it appeared that many of her fellow cooks had previously attended the 'Knife Skills' course at Wick's and been taught to hold the top of the blade with one fingertip while rapidly chopping, rather then Jess's inept sawing action. The use of a blender was a complete mystery to her, she kept trying to screw the lid on the wrong way, so that the machine would not work, and she had to be helped by the kind woman opposite her. The instructor was constantly reminding the cooks to put flan cases in the fridge to set, to stir saucepans on the range, not to forget to remove their baked flat-breads from the oven, to remember to top up their bain-maries with boiling water, to soak their chia nuts and grind their spices. If Jess had wished to imagine a morning in Hell it would have closely resembled these exhausting hours spent at the Ariadne Wick cookery school. Just as with her domestic science exam of long ago, the sun was beating in through enormous windows, stoves were going at full blast and it was clear that the perspiring Jess was way behind everyone else in ability. Jess resolved never to accept any more *Daily Mail* prizes, no matter how sought-after. It seemed that the value of this prize was £150. Jess could not imagine voluntarily spending that sum of money on an endurance test such as this cookery lesson was turning out to be, but of course, everyone else was enjoying it immensely. She discovered that the only good thing about the morning marathon was that she was not required to do any washing up, since there was a team of assistants efficiently whisking away used bowls, pans, cutlery and chopping boards and returning them perfectly clean so that everything was magically to hand as required.

At last, after a hectic three and a half hours without a break for tea or toilets - or scarcely, thought Jess, to draw breath - the cooks were permitted to sit down to sample their morning's efforts. The poached chicken was fine but Jess thought she would have preferred roast. Of course poaching was a healthier method of preparing food and the theme of the lesson was healthy cooking; Jess had expected a few exotic ingredients such as seaweed, but the chia nuts were the most outlandish item she had encountered, used as a binding agent in place of eggs. The salads were delicious, the soups and flat-breads tasty and the dark chocolate flan the best dish of all. Lastly came coffee and some sticky date sweets. The left-over food was packed into foil containers for the cooks to take home. Halfway through her complicated cross-city bus and train journey Jess realised that one of her soup containers was leaking, but luckily she had a spare plastic bag so managed to salvage the rest of the food, which Tom and his house-mates eagerly fell upon when she arrived back in Upper Clapton. Jess then headed back to Kings Cross for the return journey to Yorkshire and slept most of the way.

Martha rang the following day to find out how she had got on. Jess hadn't the heart to tell her how much of an ordeal she had found the experience so glossed over the difficult bits and stressed how helpful the assistants were and how much she had enjoyed seeing Tom and visiting the British Library. Martha asked if she would consider using any of the recipes again, but Jess was cautious in her reply, merely commenting that the dark chocolate flan with a crushed nut base rather than pastry might be worth repeating. Anything involving masses of chopping and blending was not really her style. Jess recalled her mother Dotey long ago exclaiming that the sight of Jess with a kitchen knife resembled that of 'a cow handling a musket' and according to yesterday's experience this quaint soubriquet still seemed to apply. Jess supposed that one was either born with the knack or one was not, and that to attempt to acquire any expertise would require £150 expenditure on a Knife Skills course. She could think of many better uses for that sum of money none of which necessitated enduring the rigours of a another morning at the Ariadne Wick cookery school.

Chapter 10

Alex and Zofia had found a temporary job, clearing out a house which had not been inhabited since 1981 (which, as Alex pointed out, was before either of them were born.) The house, which was located in a seaside resort in South Wales, was without essential services, since these had long ago been disconnected; however, the owner had requested that the water be turned back on, and there was apparently some unusual arrangement whereby an electric cable came in through the ceiling, from which it was possible to run one power socket. The gas supply had not yet been reinstated, and there was an ancient and massive solid fuel range which would require thorough professional restoration before any attempted use.

"We'll need to take the camping stove, an extension cable and maybe a slow cooker, as well as a kettle, crockery, cutlery, lots of cleaning stuff and all my tools," said Alex. "Do you know anyone who has a slow cooker we can borrow? And do you by any chance have a spare kettle? We're all right for camping gas, I found lots of spare cylinders clearing up after that festival. People just leave stuff behind, they can't be bothered to take it away. That's where we got our tent."

Jess rummaged in the depths of a cupboard and produced an old jug kettle. "I think Frank has a slow cooker he doesn't use. I'll ask if you can borrow it. But what are you going to do about showers?"

"They have them on the beach for the surfers, we'll go there."

Jess wondered why a house would have stood empty for almost forty years. Zofia explained that it had belonged to the late parents of a friend of hers, who now occasionally went in to light a coal fire and pick the apples from the tree in the back garden.

"That's why she doesn't want to sell the house, because she likes the old range and the apple tree. But now she's had to raise some money and the bank insists that the house is put into reasonable condition which is why she needs us to work on it."
"So – Mum; what are you and the camper van doing next week? We've got that much stuff to take, we can't possibly get the Megabus. The house is massive, it's got four bedrooms and two large downstairs living rooms; the only trouble is that you can't get into them, they're crammed full of junk. We went over for a recce when we were last in Bristol and could hardly move around the place. We'll have to chuck out loads of stuff and put down some old

mattresses I found in the attic. Better bring sleeping bags and pillow cases, Zofia put them on the list please...and a torch and candles, there's no electric lights, and of course the gas has been cut off so those old gas lamps are caput. We'll have to do our washing at the launderette on the camp-site across the road."

Jess still found it hard to comprehend the idea of a house standing empty for so long, it seemed quite wrong when there were so many homeless families in need of accommodation. Besides, the owner would still be required to pay council tax on an uninhabited property. Then a thought occurred to her.

"I hope there's no squatters, it sounds just the place for them."

"No, not even squatters could manage without water and when we visited the house was uninhabited. We had to borrow a bucket of water from the neighbour so we could flush the loo, but she said not to ask again as she doesn't get on with the owner. That's why the water's being reconnected this week."

Jess was not surprised to hear that the neighbour was somewhat aggrieved with the owner, after all, it couldn't be very pleasant living next to an empty house, no doubt with an overgrown garden and possibly vermin running about.

The old camper van was loaded to the gunwales as the three of them, plus Izzy, set off on their long journey, which went surprisingly smoothly, so that they arrived at the neglected house before four o'clock. The owner had posted Zofia the key, so they opened the door and made their way into the main room which appeared to be full of mouldering pieces of wood of all shapes and sizes. Zofia explained that the owner liked doing woodwork so often collected unusual pieces from skips and driftwood from the beach. Jess agreed that some of the bits of wood were interesting shapes but wondered why anyone would need quite so many of them. She retrieved the kettle from one of the many boxes they had brought and plugged it into the single socket so that they could have a cup of tea. There was of course no fridge but luckily there was a Co-op nearby so obtaining milk and other supplies on a daily basis would not be a problem.

Refreshed by the tea, Jess wandered through the house, dodging lumps of wood and other obstacles, with Izzy following, cautiously sniffing in all the corners. The rooms were festooned with cobwebs, and all the dilapidated fixtures and ancient furniture were coated in dust and grime. Jess quite expected to discover Miss Havisham seated in one of them. The decrepit-looking range stood forlornly in the filthy kitchen; Jess wondered when a meal had last been cooked on it. Moving into the dining room, a French window creaked open to reveal the wilderness of the garden, complete with the celebrated apple tree. Stepping carefully over brambles and through nettles in order to collect some windfalls, Jess thought the fruit must be extremely special since it was apparently one of the reasons the owner was reluctant to dispose of the house; she looked forward to tasting it. Jess wondered why the owner did not simply take a cutting and graft the apple onto a tree in her own home garden. Glancing over the low wall separating the garden from next door, Jess noted immaculate lawns, neat paths and well-maintained, colourful flowerbeds. No wonder the neighbours had been cross with the owner of the empty house, they probably considered that her wilderness spoiled their outlook. Returning to the house, mindful of obstacles and potential trip-hazard plants, Jess realised that Izzy had sensibly decided not to risk becoming entangled in the dense, low-growing jungle, and was waiting for her by the French window.

"Well, Mum; what do you think? We've got our work cut out to clear and clean this place within a month."

"I think there's probably more chance of Britain finally leaving the European Union than this house being inhabitable before Christmas! The gasmen and electricians will have to do their stuff before anyone could possibly consider living here. People expect central heating and lots of electrical sockets in every room these days, not coal fires, gas lamps and antique ranges."

Meanwhile, Zofia had already made a start, scrubbing the kitchen table so that there was somewhere to put food. She had brought a casserole which could be quickly heated up on the camping cooker. Jess had brought strawberries and yoghurt for dessert. After tea, they strolled down to the seafront, admiring the sunset over the headland. Alex had arranged the mattresses and sleeping bags, and to Jess's surprise, they all slept well.

They spent the following morning removing the various pieces of wood from the house and cleaning surfaces, before deciding on an afternoon walk to the beach. It was a lovely day, and the Bristol Channel shone bright blue. Jess found it odd to be looking at the cliffs of her native Devonshire on the opposite side of the Bristol Channel, recalling childhood trips to Ilfracombe and views across to the South Wales coast upon which she was now standing. After tea, Jess left Alex and Zofia washing up while she took Izzy for her evening stroll, choosing a path beside the perimeter of the caravan site. Rounding a bend, she heard a rumbling sound and assumed it was skateboards, but as she drew closer, she realised that there was a gang of at least a dozen young people, mostly lads but including also a few girls, all dressed alike in dark jeans and hooded tops, throwing a huge piece of wooden fence about; meanwhile several others were riving at the next panel, which they had almost succeeded in removing. At home, Jess would often challenge any vandals she came across damaging the park, but here there were so very many of them, and she felt rather intimidated. It was by now quite dark, and there was no-one else around so she decided to say nothing and walk on by, intending to report the incident to the caravan site security on her way back.

However, one of the lads stepped out, blocking Jess's path. Jess was severely outnumbered and feared that the hoodlums might try to snatch Izzy. Several members of the gang now surrounded her, hoods drawn up to partially hide their faces.

"It wasn't us that did this to the fence," said the leader, leering out of a gap in his hood in an unpleasant manner. "We just found it..."

This was obviously untrue, given that his pals were at that moment engaged in removing the next piece of fence. They gave a triumphant roar as it came away from the wooden uprights and clattered to the ground. Jess quickly decided that her best option was bravado.

"We're from Yorkshire – we don't care!" The youths all fell about laughing and let her continue towards the coastal footpath. Jess later found a security guard who had spotted the offenders on his CCTV and had already called the police; he indicated a safer, well-lit route for Jess and Izzy to take back to the main road.

Chapter 11

Back in Yorkshire, Jess was rather disconcerted to receive a call from Cecil, since she thought she had blocked him on her phone. Cecil began by asking if she had received his text messages, to which he had had no reply, so it seemed that the blocking had been only partially successful. Jess murmured something about having problems with her phone, and Cecil went on to explain the reason for his call. Another choir member, Dora, who lived quite close to Jess, had been taken into hospital after a fall and had contacted him with a request to collect various items from her ground floor flat.

"I'm not really sure why she's rung me," said Cecil, "She has a daughter who would have been far more appropriate. I was quite surprised, but I said I'd do it. But I really don't want to be rummaging through a lady's things on my own so I wondered if you would meet me at her flat to find what she needs."

Jess really did not wnt to go but felt that she could scarcely refuse this request on behalf of another choir member in distress, so agreed to be at Dora's flat in half an hour. She knew that Cecil and Dora met up from time to time to practice their melodeons together. Jess had been pleased at this development, knowing that both were lonely. However, Cecil had once complained to Jess that Dora's playing was not very good.

"All the more reason for you to continue practising with her, so she can improve," said Jess, brusquely.

Cecil was waiting outside the block of flats as Jess arrived.

"Do you have the key?" asked Jess.

"She said it was under a cup somewhere in the back garden."

They began searching the plot of grass behind the flat but there was no sign of a cup, and the only item of kitchenware to be seen was a burnt out saucepan. Then Jess noticed that Dora's bedroom window was open. She went to close it and discovered a set of keys under a cup on the window sill.

"Here's the key! Thank goodness no-one else found it, they could have walked right in and helped themselves to the TV or computer or even the melodeon!"

They went to the front door and let themselves in. Cecil had the list of things Dora required, and they made their way to the bedroom, where Jess immediately secured the window. She began searching in the chest of drawers while Cecil stared vaguely into the wardrobe.

"Eh, Jess, fancy you and I being in a bedroom together!" said Cecil.

Jess ignored this remark and carried on with her rummaging. None of Dora's requested items seemed to be in the obvious place, which was perplexing. She looked around the room, wondering where Dora kept her underwear, when her eye fell on the red electric blanket control.

"The blanket's been on all this time! Lucky there wasn't a fire!"

Jess rushed across to switch off the electric blanket, accidentally brushing against Cecil's arm as she did.

"I know a way we could warm up this bed..." said Cecil suggestively.

"Let's just concentrate on the job in hand!" screamed Jess. She was bitterly regretting having agreed to come, since it now appeared that Cecil was using it as a pretext to be alone with her. Jess had found only half the things Dora wanted, but was determined to leave the flat as quickly as possible. She spotted an address book on the table.

"Ah! Her daughter's address is here. It's in Manchester. I'll ring her and ask her to come over to sort everything out. Hospitals always want to speak to the next of kin. You say you don't know why Dora gave your details, but perhaps yours was the only number she could remember at the time, or was the last number rung on her phone."

"Eh, but I could never fancy Dora..." mused Cecil. Jess didn't reply. She felt like slapping him. They reached the front door and locked it.

"I can take these things to the hospital and give Dora her keys to pass on to her daughter. There's no need for us to do anything further. We've fastened the window, turned off the blanket and the flat is now safe and secure." Jess rushed off before Cecil could think of making any further inappropriate remarks.

Jess telephoned Dora's daughter who said she would visit as soon as she could. Jess then set off for the hospital, where she found Dora lying forlornly on a bed in a side ward. She smiled as Jess entered. "I've brought your things, well, as many as I could find. You seem to have a lot of handbags so I hope this is the right one..."

"Yes, the one with my purse. Ah, you found the address book too!"

"I rang your daughter and she'll come as soon as she can. Do you know how long you are likely to be in here?"

"They haven't said, but I'll need to see the physiotherapist so it's not likely I'll be out very soon. It was such a silly thing, I slipped outside the shop. People were so kind and I didn't have to wait long for the ambulance. You got into the flat OK then?"

"Well, it was rather an escapade, and I don't think it's wise to leave your keys on the windowsill - anyone could get them!"

"I always do, so I know I can never lock myself out. They should be under a cup. I only meant to be out a short time..."

"Even so, it's not a good idea to have the window open on the ground floor, it's lucky you haven't been burgled, these opportunist thieves go round looking for open windows and could easily have climbed in. Anyway, I've shut it now."

Jess decided not to mention Cecil's inappropriate behaviour to Dora. She herself had been seriously considering leaving the choir in order to avoid meeting him, until she thought better of it; after all, why should she be obliged to give up something she enjoyed simply because of the antics of an idiotic man? Jess decided to ask one of the men in the choir to have a word with Cecil about how members were expected to treat one other with respect, and how the choir should provide a safe and welcoming environment for all. If anyone had to leave, it really should be creepy Cecil, not long-standing member Jess. She telephoned a sensible man who sang with the basses, who agreed with her about the inappropriateness of Cecil's behaviour, kindly promising to speak to him on the matter of respect for all choir members in general and Jess in particular.

Chapter 12

As Jess walked down the road with Izzy she came across a set of temporary traffic lights and a team of workmen busily raising the level of the pavement, while other were painting large Bus Stop signs on the road. The workmen explained that it had been decreed that all bus services should accommodate disabled people, including those routes which operated infrequently such as the one which came up Jess's road, which ran once every two hours during the day and not at all at night or on Sundays. The raised pavement levels would enable wheelchair users to board the buses more easily while the bright yellow paint would clearly indicate that no cars should be parked in the surrounding area. Jess applauded this action, since inclusivity was so important. Returning home just before the onset of a heavy downpour, she made a cup of tea, glad to be indoors. Then she heard someone in her next-door neighbour's yard shouting furiously and knocking on the back door. Looking out Jess saw the tall, dark, curly-haired youngish man to whom she had complained about noise, now dripping wet and desperate.

"Abby! Let me in! Abby – am I the father of your child?"

Jess rushed to her shed and retrieved an old umbrella, which had a broken spoke and was used only on dog walks, but still afforded some shelter, and handed this over the wall. The drenched man smiled at her gratefully.

"Would you like a cup of tea? I've just boiled the kettle."

"I'd love a hot brew! Milk and two sugars, please!"

Jess filled a mug with scalding tea, stirred in the sugar and handed it to the man in Abby's yard, now sheltering under the broken umbrella. She noticed he was shivering. Her umbrella had evidently arrived too late to prevent his clothing from becoming completely soaked.

"Would you like to come in and warm up? I've lit the fire."
"No, thank you; Abby and I have stuff we need to sort out."

Jess returned to her kitchen, while the man resumed his persistent shouting at the window and fruitless banging on the door. There was loud music playing in the next-door house, so evidently Abby was intent on drowning out the man's entreaties. Eventually he gave up and came into Jess's yard to return the mug and umbrella.

"Thanks for the tea, I'd better be going now but I'll try again later..."

The man made his way down the back street, while Jess hoped that he and Abby could resolve their differences without too many more

48

such noisy episodes. Jess preferred to live in a peaceful neighbourhood free from on-going domestic dramas.

The following week, as Jess made her way into the village, she observed a number of notices fastened to lamp posts. On reading one, Jess was amazed to discover that the notice announced the intention of discontinuing the bus service from the end of the month.

"But they've only just spent all this time and money raising the pavement level in order to accommodate wheelchairs on the buses! Why on earth bother with that if the service is to be discontinued?" asked Jess of no-one in particular, since naturally Izzy did not respond. An elderly man passing by heard her cry of astonishment.

"'Appen the left hand doesn't know that t'right hand's doing. I've been using this bus for twenty year now, and I've no idea how I'm going to get my shopping, can't afford a taxi..."

"I suppose they think everyone orders online these days. But lots of us still like to go out and choose things ourselves, and to see people. It's another step towards everyone becoming isolated and lonely."

"Tha's reet there, lass; my son's been trying to persuade me to move into sheltered accommodation, and I've allus said to him, no I'm fine where I am, let me stay in my own home. But now it looks like I might have to move if they knock off this bus. Tha'll either 'ave to have a car or be very fit to live down this street now. Or be very handy with computers."

Jess read the notice again, but there did not appear to be any right of appeal against the bus company's decision. The road rose sharply beyond her terrace, too steep for most people carrying heavy shopping bags. So the elderly folk would have to move away and the rich mix of the village community would be diminished.

Returning home, Jess picked up her post, and was alarmed to discover a letter from the council marked Important. She opened it with trepidation, wondering what could possibly be the matter, since she was not in arrears with her council tax and so far as she she was aware had not placed any illegal items in her wheelie bin. The letter stated that a complaint had been received regarding the playing of loud music and the sound of raised voices coming from her address, and that the council's Directorate of Neighbourhood Services would not hesitate to take further action if this warning not to behave in an inconsiderate manner should go unheeded. Jess was astonished, and not a little upset, since she believed that she always tried to behave in a neighbourly and considerate manner. She reached for the phone to ring the council in an attempt to discover who had complained and what exactly it was that could have prompted the complaint. As usual, the council's contact centre telephonist was unable to connect her to the correct department, explaining that all officers were very busy, and no-one was currently available, but that someone would call her back in due course. Jess suspected that no-one from the council would call her back since they hardly ever did. Then she remembered that local councillors, the elected representatives, did not have to go through the contact centre and be fobbed off with excuses, but could get straight through the various departments. Councillors had a direct line to senior officers so Jess telephoned her local Berringden Brow ward representative, Cllr. Morag Bentley. Cllr. Morag, in her usual efficient manner, promised to get to the bottom of the matter and let Jess know the outcome.

Before teatime, a man grandly announcing himself as the Deputy Director of the Neighbourhood Services Directorate was on the phone to Jess, informing her that a complaint about noise had indeed been raised, he was not at liberty to say by whom due to Data Protection considerations, but that unfortunately, on checking the complaint, the letter appeared to have been sent to Jess's address in error. It should have gone to the house next door.

"Well, that's simply not good enough!" exclaimed an angry Jess. "I'm a law-abiding pensioner who has been really upset by the whole incident, while the person to whom it actually applies is unaware of any complaint about their behaviour."

The official said he could only apologise and would ensure that the complaint was expunged from Jess's records. Jess was relieved to hear that she would no longer be recorded as being a bad neighbour or have any permanent stain against her character.

Later that evening Jeff telephoned to tell Jess he had not after all been appointed to the position with the office of the Police Commissioner. Jess was concerned that this might be because of her own activities with CND and the League Against Cruel Sports in the 1980s, which Jeff had been obliged to disclose to the authorities, but Jeff said it was probably because as a septuagenarian white man he would be regarded as 'pale, male and stale', and that the successful applicant would in all probability turn out to be someone very different, by whose appointment the authority could demonstrate its commitment to diversity.

Chapter 13

Jess was pleased that the Film Club at the local library was about to start up again for the new season. This was run by Ben, the librarian on whom she had had a crush some years ago. Jess had later come to realise that this was part of a menopausal syndrome, and once she had emerged from that unsettling stage of life, common sense had prevailed and she had been back to her usual sensible self. Ben's choice of film was not always to Jess's taste, but she felt that it was important to have her cinematic horizons expanded, since Ben's selections made a change from her usual preferred viewing of rom-coms and period dramas. Last time, Ben had shown the French film *The War of the Buttons* which Jess had enjoyed despite it having subtitles with which she sometimes struggled. She had to remember to take her glasses with her when foreign films were being shown. Ben had asked her afterwards what she had thought of the film, and during their conversation it had struck Jess that she often enjoyed films which featured children in leading roles.

"Yes, it reminded me a bit of *Moonrise Kingdom*."

"Ah; you liked that - a Wes Anderson film...."

"*The Hunt for the Wilderpeople,* that was very good too. And my favourite film as a child was *Whistle Down the Wind.*"

"Of course, that was made just over the hill in Burnley."

Jess had been taken to see *Whistle Down the Wind* as a child in Devon by her mother, who was a fan of young Hayley Mills. Set in black and white Lancashire, Jess could never then guess that she would visit such a faraway place, let alone live nearby. Anything north of Bristol was regarded as 'up-country' - a bleak region too far away for most Devonians to even imagine. Yet for the past thirty years Jess had been living only half an hour away from Burnley.

This month's offering was to be *Langrishe, Go Down* with a young Judi Dench and Jeremy Irons, plus a screenplay by Harold Pinter, a film which Jess would probably not have chosen but was interested to see since she had many years ago been cast in a Pinter play at Tiverton Grammar School. This work, entitled *Night School,* had Jess playing the leading role of Sally. The plot centres around a man returning to his elderly aunts' home after a spell in prison, only to find that they have rented his room to a sweet young games teacher who secretly doubles a night-club hostess. The unsuspecting aunts believe that she is studying at Night School but their nephew has his suspicions. Jess, in the throes of her crush, had previously told Ben all about this, the pinnacle of her am-dram career. According to the internet, the play was stated to feature many aspects of Comedy of Menace and Jess thought the same might well be said of *Langrishe. ..* but really without very much comedy and more of an accent on the menace, since the controlling professor Jeremy Irons character isolated young Judi Dench's Imogen from her sisters. Jess recalled that she could take Pinter only in small doses and was relieved when the film ended so she could return home to Izzy.

Tom announced that he was coming up from London to Yorkshire for his birthday. Luckily November 1st this year fell during the schools' half term so all the local attractions were still open. Jess wanted to take a trip into the Standedge Tunnel on the Huddersfield Narrow canal, the highest, longest and deepest tunnel on the English canal network, so she booked the tickets. Tom arrived very late on the night of Hallowe'en and made his weary way to the small attic bedroom. The next morning, he appeared refreshed from the shower, commenting on the pleasant smell of the tea tree shampoo.

"But we haven't got any tea tree shampoo," said Jess.

" You have, that green bottle to the left of the taps.."

"Ah, yes; that's actually Izzy's dog shampoo; but I don't suppose she'll mind you using it."

Upon arrival at Standedge, Jess was disappointed to see that there was still a large amount of Hallowe'en tat festooned around the café, with cobwebs, bats and witches hanging everywhere so that it was impossible to carry a tray across the room without knocking against some tawdry item. Jess pointed out that November 1st was actually All Saints Day so that the decorations had outstayed their welcome. The boat was no better, with various plastic apparitions dangling from the ceiling. There were hard hats on the seats, which the guide, explained were for use on deck only, and passengers were not to worry about the state of the boat's Perspex roof, which was perfectly sound. Once inside the tunnel, Jess was amazed at just how narrow it was, barely the width of the boat. Stuart the guide recounted the history and the reasons for its building, three difficult miles hacked through the Pennine millstone grit to Diggle, in order to transport heavy cargoes, chiefly wool. The canal had replaced the arduous Pennine pack horse trail and had been the M62 of its day. When they were deep into the tunnel Stuart warned the passengers that he was about to turn off the light so that the boat would be in utter darkness.

"You literally cannot see your hand in front of your face!"

Jess found the complete blackness unnerving until someone brushed against one of the plastic ghosts which immediately made an eerie noise and lit up, startling everyone and causing several gasps and shrieks. Stuart switched the light back on and pointed out the marks on the tunnel walls, put there for the benefit of men legging their way through by candle light, so that they would have known how much further they had to go. Professional leggers were paid one shilling and sixpence per journey, more if the loads were heavy. Since there was no tow-path through the tunnel the horses had to be led over the hill to rejoin their boats at the other entrance. (Jess at first thought this was 'on the Lancashire side' but when the tunnel was constructed the village of Diggle was in West Yorkshire, and the area was not incorporated into the Red Rose county until after the controversial local government reforms of 1974. Jess and Zofia had once visited Saddleworth Museum where the attendant had assured them that many local people resented having been switched into Lancashire and still regarded themselves as bona fide West Riding residents.)

Back at the café, Tom thanked Jess for the unusual birthday treat. A text message from Alex prompted them to return home, where Alex was preparing for a firework party. His plan was to climb up the hill and along a footpath to the top of Scout Rocks and light the village beacon, usually only lit for events of national importance such as Jubilees or sightings of Armadas. Alex and Zofia had brought with them a quantity of fireworks plus a sack of firewood, copious liquid refreshments, a box of matches and a bottle of white spirit to get the fire going on this soggy night. Zofia said that in Poland people lit candles in the graveyards for All Saints Day, so Alex was actually adapting a widespread European tradition of lighting up the darkness.

"There's quite a few people coming, Mum, I told them to meet here."

Jess was aware that the house was not very tidy and she had her washing, including some rather dilapidated underwear, hanging on the creel in the kitchen. Not knowing of Alex's plan until the last minute, she had not had time to tidy up. Meanwhile, people were trooping in wearing wet weather gear, head torches and heavy shoes, carrying yet more cans of beer. At one point someone arrived with a collie dog, so Jess hastily ushered him out again before Izzy noticed, not wanting a dog fight in her front room. A tall, saturnine, young man suddenly appeared at the front door wielding an axe, which somewhat startled Jess until she realised that he was going to help Alex chop wood. She directed him to the back lane where Alex was supervising preparations. The tall young man ducked under Jess's washing and was soon enthusiastically splitting firewood. Jess then found her front room was full, with yet more people congregating in the kitchen. She went to make a cup of tea and discovered one visitor had made himself quite at home, boiling the kettle and filling a flask.

"Who are you?" asked Jess. The man said he was Chris from the Sixth Form College he and Tom had attended more than twenty years previously. Alex had gone to a lot of trouble rounding up as many of Tom's friends as still lived locally .

Izzy was sprawled on her favourite chair, she always enjoyed meeting new people so was quite unfazed by all the visitors, while Jess was rather anxious about the tramping of so many muddy boots and shoes through the house. At last everyone was assembled and the party marched up the road in the rain towards the rocks. Jess elected to go to the bottom of the hill from where the beacon would be clearly visible, rather than climb the steep path and be obliged to slide about on wet stones. Alex promised to send her a text when the fire was lit so she would not have to wait about in the rain any longer than necessary.

Despite the damp conditions, the beacon blazed clearly above the village of Berringden Brow, the fireworks soared into the night sky and Tom's birthday was duly celebrated. Later, when the fire had died away, Jess heard the revellers returning back down the hill, and went to the front door to meet them. Alex handed her several bags of spent fireworks and empty beer cans, asking her to dispose of them since the party was about to carry on elsewhere; he assured her that nothing had been left on the rocks and no-one passing along the footpath would be able to tell that the place had been the scene of a unique and successful celebration.

Chapter 14

Jess, out with Izzy on their usual morning walk, was surprised to come across a young couple apparently trying to stash a tent in the hedge at the end of the playing field. It was late autumn and most of the leaves in the hedge had disappeared, so the tent was clearly visible. The lad was vainly attempting to shove the frame deeper into the sparse greenery, while the girl, who looked very young, stood shivering and silently looking on.

"What are you doing?" asked Jess. The young man explained that they needed to hide the tent while they went into the village. They could not carry it around the shops and were unable to think of anywhere better to put it.

Jess felt sure that the tent would be stolen if left in the field, since it was far from hidden. The corner they had chosen was frequented by drug users, as evidenced by the empty cannabis packs strewn about.

"Well, you can leave the tent in my shed if you like, it will be quite safe there. I don't keep it locked as it's almost full of old junk already so you could collect it whenever you wanted." Jess led the way across the road and into the back lane. She showed the couple where her shed was located and watched while the young man stowed the tent inside. The girl stood still silently shivering in the lane.

"How long have you been sleeping rough?" asked Jess. The lad replied that they had been homeless for six weeks. Despite Jess trying to include her in the conversation, the girl still said nothing.

"Six weeks - camping in all that rain and cold!" Jess shook her head. "What are you names? I'm Jess, by the way."

"I'm Dan and this is Ellie." Jess wondered if Ellie was mute. She had not uttered a single word during their encounter, leaving all the talking to Dan. Jess went on to enquire how old they were, and again Dan answered, saying that he was eighteen and Ellie was sixteen.

"Surely you're classed as vulnerable, so can't Social Services help?"

"Ellie is actually under the social but they don't do nuffin," said Dan. "I've got a Probation officer, but he's really stretched so can't help."

"But what can have brought you to this? Where are your families?"

"Mine's here in't village but I don't like to rely on them. Besides, I've had serious issues with mi mother's partner. Ellie's got no family, they're abusive, so I'm all the family she has now. I've applied for an 'ouse for the both of us but there's no saying when we'll get one."

"Do you have sufficient bedding?" asked Jess. Dan said they only had one quilt between them so Jess offered to look out an old sleeping bag she was sure she had in a cupboard somewhere, and put it by the tent for their use.

Ellie stood still shivering, the hood of her anorak pulled round her pale face, her thin legs encased in skinny jeans which would not provide much warmth. Jess was just wondering if she should offer them a warm drink or the use of her bathroom, when Dan emerged from the shed.

"That's very kind of you; we're off now to see if my mum's at home."

Jess was relieved to hear this and hoped that some sort of family reconciliation might occur so that they could have a roof over their heads. The couple did not return that evening to collect the tent so she began to believe that all must now be well with Dan and Ellie.

The next day Jess was again out with Izzy, when they came across a grey heron standing stock still in the playing field pond. Jess was reaching for her phone in order to take a picture when she heard a distant commotion, Dan's voice, using appalling language, directed at Ellie. The heron, thus disturbed, flapped its wings and flew off. The tirade continued, and Jess saw Ellie dash past on the path the other side of the pond. Tears were streaming down her face, and she was shouting incoherently. Ellie rushed off into the woods, screaming something about the railway line. Jess realised that Dan and another girl were running some way behind, Dan still f-ing and blinding. Jess recalled that in her youth one could be 'had up' for disturbing the Sunday peace in this manner.

"Dan!" called Jess. "Please don't use language like that! Ellie seems very upset and anyway you should speak to everyone with respect!"

Dan and the other girl gave up their futile chase and approached Jess.

"It's her that's wound Dan up," said the girl. "She's threatening to put herself on the railway track cos she knows that's how Dan's uncle ended up. That's what's upset him!"

"Yeah, I tried to stop my uncle but I couldn't so I literally had to lift his head and body separately off the tracks. Now Ellie's threatening to do t'same, and she knows that will set me off like nothing else..."

"She's clearly vulnerable, and no disrespect to you Dan, but surely someone more responsible should be looking out for her. Does she go to school? What about a Social Worker, if she's in council care?"

"Nay, she doesn't go to school. As for a Social Worker, she's got one but they don't really bother. I've got to go soon, we stayed at my mum's last night so I've texted her to come and help look for Ellie."

Jess knew the trains ran only once an hour on Sundays and there was not one due for forty minutes. She hoped Ellie would soon be found.

"OK Dan, perhaps you'd like to collect your tent tomorrow if you're back at your mum's now?"

"Nay I'm up I'm court tomorrow morning, on an assault charge. I knocked out the man who pulled a knife on my mum, had to defend her, didn't I, and now I'm in court over it."

Jess was beginning to think she had inadvertently become involved in an episode of "This is England" (The gritty 90s Shane Meadows film followed by a number of television drama sequels.) She watched Dan and his friend walk back towards the road where they expected to meet Dan's mother. Jess felt that she ought to do something, but there was obviously no way she would be able to catch up with Ellie, who by now would have a considerable head start over her pursuers.

Jess returned home, and thought that she should ring the council out of hours number for advice. After all, Ellie was in council care, so maybe a duty social worker should come out to look for her. Jess eventually got through to someone at Berringden Council, who asked her for Ellie's description, then told her to hold while she found someone appropriate to ask. The official returned to the phone and said that there was nothing anyone could do on a Sunday, except look out for Ellie on CCTV.

"Are you certain that's all? Surely the council is in loco parentis. Haven't you got a duty Social Worker there?"

"This is the out of hours emergency number with only a skeleton staff so there's no further action we can take today."

Jess was quite shocked at this response. She hoped Dan and his fellow searchers had found Ellie and that all would be well. She went outside and listened for any sounds but all was peaceful. Jess fetched Izzy's lead and together they walked the half mile to the railway bridge; Jess looked up and down the track but could see no-one. Jess resolved to try to contact Social Services the following day when she could perhaps expect a more positive response to the plight of a vulnerable young girl living rough with a lad who was up on an assault charge. What if Dan were to be found guilty and sent to a Young Offenders Institution? It seemed that Ellie would have no-one looking out for her. Jess was concerned for her future.

Accordingly, on Monday, Jess tried to get through to the Social Services but was unable to get past the council call-centre answerphone system. She held on for half an hour without speaking to a real person so eventually hung up. She then decided to email Berringden Council, and received the standard acknowledgement message by way of reply. Then a thought struck her, that since Dan was up in court, the local paper might have sent a reporter to cover the proceedings. She rang the office of the *Berringden Bugle*, where a bored sounding journalist told her that the paper no longer covered court reports as a matter of course, sending someone only if the case concerned something of substantial public interest, and Dan's assault case would not fall into this category. The court sent the paper a list of the outcomes of cases heard but this usually took three weeks to arrive. Jess concluded the court must use a messenger with a forked stick going by the scenic route rather than email. Surely even a carrier pigeon would be quicker. Jess felt she had tried her best and that there was nothing further she could do. Meanwhile the tent and bedding remained in her shed.

The Film Club screening this month was *Tulip Fever*, which again featured Judi Dench, this time playing a much older character, an abbess in Seventeenth Century Amsterdam, who has a tulip garden in the middle of her convent. The story of the affair between a young married woman and the artist hired to paint a portrait of the woman and her elderly husband took place during the period when tulip bulbs were being traded for astronomical prices. The story also featured sex, drunkenness, Eastern spices, devout religion, the intervention of the Press Gang, a conniving and thoroughly unprofessional doctor and a complicated baby-swap plot. A real romp, which Jess enjoyed very much.

Chapter 15

Jess arrived at the church hall in plenty of time to set up her bookstall to find that the hall was already busy with preparations for the Advent Fair. Bags and boxes of all descriptions were being unloaded in the car park and carried into the hall; Jess noted that the stall-holders were mainly women and the bag carriers their dutiful husbands. The afternoon was dull and it was beginning to rain. Jess hoped this would not deter people from coming.

"Ah, Jess; I've put you in the Creative Corner, over there next to Moira with her twigs, you're on table 21" said Helen, the church warden, appearing from behind a roped off area where several people were struggling to erect the tent which was to serve as Santa's grotto.

Jess made her way across the hall, trying to find her table but could not locate it. Moira was arranging her jam-jars of sparsely decorated painted twigs; Jess thought they looked rather bleak and doubted that many Yorkshire folk would pay good money for them but Moira evidently subscribed to the dictum that 'less is more'. Jess then realised that Moira and the twigs had overflowed onto table 21 as well as their own allocated stall, table 22.

Jess began to move the intrusive twig jars over onto table 22. Moira looked most annoyed.

"I really need more space! How does Helen expect we **artists** to manage with these pokey stalls? I simply can't exhibit my work to the best effect unless I have an extra table! Anyway, this is meant to be Creative Corner but you've just brought a load of books, surely you belong over there - next to the jumble!" said Moira.
"I wrote the books, so I did create them. Anyway, I'm just following Helen's instructions. I'm on Table 21."

It did not take very long for Jess to arrange her books on the table, and since there was still ten minutes before the fair officially opened she thought she would tour the hall and look at everyone else's stalls.

"Ah, Jess; have some mulled wine! It's my own blackberry, last year's vintage, and I've put some special local herbs in it." Jess approached Pam's table with some trepidation, wondering just what the special local herbs might be. She sipped cautiously, but the drink was warming and tasted fine. Jess hoped that she would suffer no ill effects later.

Back at Santa's grotto, the tent was listing alarmingly, and the Vicar's husband was endeavouring to prop it up with a broom, while Vicar Evelyn herself was busy untangling a chain of fairy-lights.

"Jess, can you see if there's an extension lead in the cupboard, I doubt these will reach..."

Jess opened the cupboard where the cleaning things were kept and discovered a small boy crouched among the dustpans and brushes. She recognised Helen's young son.

"What are you doing in here Jimmy?"

"Mum said to make myself scarce because she was so busy, so I decided to hide until she missed me."

"Well, can you see an extension lead anywhere? They need it for Santa's fairy-lights."

Jimmy rummaged in the depths of the cupboard and produced the extension cable.

"That's good, maybe you could take it over to the Vicar, she needs to get those lights up and Santa safely installed before all the little kids arrive to see him."

Jimmy emerged from the cupboard and made his way to the Grotto, which was still leaning dangerously to starboard. Jess returned to Creative Corner, where Moira was still fussing with her twigs.

"Ah Jess, you're back; I don't suppose you have any spare change, do you? I seem not to have brought very much and people always tend to hand me twenty-pound notes."

Jess fished five pound coins from the biscuit tin where she kept her change and gave them to Moira, who looked rather annoyed.

"Is that really all you can spare?" she grumbled, grudgingly handing Jess a five-pound note.

"Well, yes; as you say, people always give us notes and the change has to last all afternoon." Jess noted that Moira was selling her creations for twelve pounds fifty a jar, which she considered to be a ridiculous amount. Jess's books were reasonably priced at seven pounds.

The fair began, and hordes of parishioners arrived, some with push-chairs, wheel-chairs and dogs on leads, so that the hall soon became quite crowded and traffic was at a standstill. Jess decided to turn this to her advantage, since she had a captive audience in front of her stall. She began announcing the books as great stocking-fillers, wonderful presents for any reader, and - addressing the women - what better way to relax after doing all that cooking and finally getting rid of the visitors than to put your feet up with a good book? With couples, Jess spoke to the men, assuring them that they would be in Her good books if they bought their partners one of Jess's. People laughed, and Jess was soon doing a roaring trade. However, prospective buyers leaning over to inspect the books often became entangled with an overhanging twig from the adjacent stall, which annoyed Moira considerably, but Jess thought it was really her own fault for not positioning her jars sufficiently far back from the edge of her table...

The afternoon wore on, and Jess noticed that there were fewer people entering the hall, and those that came in were dripping wet. Damp-looking men in high-viz jackets - the local flood wardens - appeared with anxious looks on their faces, grabbed a cup of tea and rushed out again. The church was right next to the river, and had been flooded the previous year. There had been various flood prevention works since, but these were as yet untested and it was not certain that they would be sufficient to hold back the flow. Meanwhile, disaster was looming for Santa, where the temporary repair measures had evidently started to fail so that the Grotto was collapsing around the big man and his customers. A sobbing child emerged, rubbing his head and screaming that he had been hit by a broom. Santa himself attempted to follow but became entangled in the sagging strings of fairy-lights. A muttered tirade of unseasonable language ensued. Jess rushed to help him, thinking that it was a good thing no young children were in earshot, as the lead flood warden re-entered the hall, stood on a chair and shouted.

"T' river's rising fast, flood siren's about to go off, so you must all leave immediately!"

Jess managed to disentangle Santa and returned to her stall, where she scooped the few remaining books back into her boxes. She noticed that Moira had sold very few of the twigs; Jess wondered if she should offer to stay and help Moira pack up, but decided against it. Hastily wrapping plastic bags around the book boxes, she made her way to the car-park. The river was in full spate and appeared about to burst its banks, so Jess was glad she lived up the hill. Luckily, the flood works held, millions of pounds evidently well spent, so that the river was contained and the Berringden Brow parishioners' Christmas was saved.

Chapter 16

As Christmas approached, Jess was intrigued to see that a small fir tree growing beside the cycle path had been decorated overnight with a colourful array of baubles and tinsel. A luggage label tied to one of the branches explained that this had been done in honour of the anonymous decorator's late sister. Various neighbours, joggers, cyclists and dog walkers admired it as they passed. However, the following morning Jess was dismayed to discover that the tree had been stripped bare of its decorations with only the luggage label forlornly remaining. A group of local people were standing around discussing the Scrooge-like outrage.

"It'll just be kids," said one of the dog walkers.

Jess disagreed. "If it was kids, they'd have simply thrown the baubles around, but these have been systematically removed. Someone must have come prepared, with scissors and a large bag, since there's no trace of any remaining."

"But who on earth would do such a thing?" asked Pam. "Especially as it says the decorations were to commemorate someone's dead sister. The mentality of some people..."

"Anyway, we can't let them win," said Jess. "I'm sure I have some tree decorations left over, and if we each contribute a few we can replace the stolen ones."

Everyone nodded and said that they would fetch their spare baubles in order to restore the fir to its former festive glory. Later, when Jess and Izzy checked on the tree, it was ablaze with ornaments and tinsel of every hue. Jess hoped the mysterious bauble thief would not return, after all, Christmas decorations were cheap enough, so there was really no need to steal them from the community. Jess recalled a summer initiative in her previous village, when the playing field committee had organised an assault course for the children's Sunday Funday. It had taken all day Saturday to prepare, and a rumour had been heard that the local yobs were planning to dismantle it overnight in order to sabotage the event. Two committee members had volunteered to camp out overnight in order to guard the assault course. However, it would be impossible to keep a constant eye on the tree, since camping out would be impracticable in December.

Tom was due to reach Berringden Brow at teatime on Christmas Eve, and Jess was fretting that his train might be delayed or cancelled so that he would miss his connection and be stranded at Retford or some other unlikely place over the festive season. Her worries proved groundless when Tom arrived on schedule. Alex and Zofia soon turned up, laden with food and presents, so Jess was able to breathe a sigh of relief, with her family complete. Nick came in later, having as usual been sorting out people's problems until the very last moment. He had a bag full of festive offerings from grateful clients, including two tins of biscuits, three boxes of chocolates, a brightly patterned jumper and a couple of garish shirts which Jess knew he was unlikely ever to wear.

Christmas Day was sunny, so after their breakfast and the present opening the family set off for their traditional walk.

"Let's go up Scout Rocks and along the top and back," said Alex. Accordingly, they made their way up the hill and onto the footpath which ran along the top of the rocks. The Berringden Valley was spread below, bathed in weak winter sunshine. Suddenly Alex motioned the others to stop.

"Look, there's a kestrel on that branch!" They watched and waited until the kestrel flew off, no doubt in search of its Christmas lunch. The family continued their walk through fields and down the steep path and until finally joining a track leading to a remote farmhouse. This was no longer a working farm but had been converted into a luxurious AirBnB for people with 4x4 vehicles which could negotiate the access lane. These days there was evidently more money in renting out up-market guest accommodation than in upland farming. A small assortment of traditional breed hens scratched about in the yard, perhaps providing guests with the illusion of rural self sufficiency. Jess had no doubt that the house would be on spring water and have a septic tank rather than being connected to the main drains. A significant number of isolated farms high up in the valley still boasted a private water supply, and people often claimed that living in these remote farms and cottages and drinking spring water all their lives meant that they had never ailed a day. No chlorine or fluoride for them.

Back home, Tom, Alex and Zofia soon had the celebratory meal under way, Tom seeing to the chicken while the others had brought an already prepared exotic tagine dish by way of a contrast. Jess had peeled all the vegetables the previous day, so everyone was soon gathered around the table pulling crackers. Jess was anxious to stress these were left over from the previous Christmas, as now it was considered not to be 'green' to buy crackers containing plastic items.

"Oh those kill-joys!" said Tom. "Anyway, we can recycle plastic nowadays, can't we? So what's the harm? I've got a miniature pack of cards, so I suppose they might come in useful for a very small person playing patience."

Jess had a tiny model aeroplane, while Zofia found a fortune-telling fish in her cracker. Nick had the most useful item, a key-ring, while Alex discovered to his disappointment that his cracker was empty save for a paper hat.

"I'm already helping to save the planet, there's nowt in mine!"

Nick had a copy of a newspaper containing a lengthy quiz, which kept them occupied for most of the evening until it was time to watch the *Gavin and Stacey Christmas Special*. Jess took Izzy across the road for her night-time constitutional, and returned to find her sons washing up.

"This is wonderful - I've hardly had to do a thing!" said Jess. "It's so much more fun to all go for a walk and have a fairly easy-to-prepare meal rather than me being stuck by the oven all day basting a turkey!"

"You deserve it, Mum!" said Alex, hugging her. "All those years you made Christmas dinner for us, and now it's our turn to repay you."

"Yes," said Tom, fishing a sprout leaf from the bottom of the sink. "It's been a classic Christmas – and we're all still speaking to each other!"

Chapter 17

New Year's Day brought a surprise, in that the tent belonging to the homeless young couple, Dan and Ellie, had at last been removed from Jess's shed. Looking over the wall into the playing field, Jess observed a small camp fire and the dim outline of the tent in the corner where she had first encountered the pair several weeks previously. She was therefore not surprised to hear clattering in her yard the following morning. Dan was putting the tent back into the shed, while Ellie was her usual silent self, standing watching as Dan stowed their belongings. Jess then noticed an older man loitering on the other side of her gate.

"Hiya!" said Dan, cheerily. "Hope you don't mind, we're still in need of somewhere to keep our stuff. And Ellie's got this bag of clothes, is it all right if we leave that as well?"

"I suppose so, if you can find room for it," said Jess. "Who's that chap over there, is he with you?"

"Yeah, that's mi uncle, Mick. He's staying with us just now."

"It must be a dreadful squash with three of you in that small tent. Why is he homeless?"

"He's had a bit of trouble, so I said I'd look after him, being family." Jess recalled that one of Dan's uncles had committed suicide on the railway track, and now here was yet another troubled relative. She remembered Dan had mentioned a court case the last time they met.

"What happened about your court case? Assault, wasn't it?"

"Oh, yeah, the case got postponed, not sure when it's being heard now... Anyway Jess, we must be off, got to meet someone in the village. Probably be back again tonight to collect our stuff, we'll try not to make too much noise so as not to disturb you, thanks again." Jess wondered where they had been over the past weeks but realised that Dan was not keen to prolong their chat so refrained from asking.

That evening the trio returned to fetch the tent and Ellie's bag. As they set off down the path to the field Jess noticed that Ellie was lagging a little behind so called to her.

"Ellie, could you come here a minute please." The girl turned back and looked at Jess with her usual blank expression.

"I just wanted to ask, do you have everything you need? Would you like to come in and use the bathroom and have a shower?"

Ellie nodded and returned to the yard. She still had not said a word. Jess showed her the bathroom and indicated how to work the shower. She handed Ellie a towel and left.

Jess was making herself a cup of tea when there was a loud knocking at the back door, which opened to reveal a cross-looking Dan.

"Is Ellie here? We can't find her."

"Yes, she's just using the bathroom, I offered her a shower. She'll be down in a minute."

"Oh. Well tell her to come straight down to the field as soon as she's finished. We've put the tent up so we're turning in soon."

Jess noted Dan's stern expression and it crossed her mind that he might well be the sort of controlling boyfriend who did not allow his girlfriend to do anything without his permission. She wondered if her kindly-meant gesture in offering Ellie the use of her bathroom might have inadvertently caused her trouble. Ellie then reappeared wearing a different set of clothes and with her long hair still wet. Jess suggested she might like to use her hair-drier, since it would not be advisable to go out in to the cold night air with wet hair, and Ellie accepted, but before she could finish drying her hair an even more stony-faced Dan was again knocking on the door. He glared at Ellie, who meekly picked up her bag and followed Dan down the path.

By now, alarm bells were ringing in Jess's mind. Ellie was sixteen, nominally in council care, homeless, and sharing a tent with a controlling lad and his much older uncle. Her fears were further increased the next morning when several of the local dog-walking group reported hearing shouting coming from the tent, definitely the young man's voice, directing a tirade of bad language at Ellie. The tent was pitched right next to the path some of the walkers took, and someone passing by as the tent flap opened had seen that the older man was sleeping in the middle, which everyone agreed was rather odd. Surely Dan should be between his uncle and girlfriend? Meanwhile another kind neighbour, Damien, had arrived with bags of food and flasks of hot drinks, moved by the plight of homeless people on the doorstep. After eating their donated breakfast, the trio came to stow their belongings in Jess's shed. Jess asked Ellie if she would like to use the bathroom again. Ellie glanced fearfully at Dan, but Jess quickly intervened.

"You know, Dan, it's one thing for men to pee in the woods, but it's much more difficult for women to manage, which is why I've asked Ellie in. I'm sure that any considerate young man would understand."

Dan nodded, rather reluctantly Jess thought, so Ellie scuttled indoors.

"Be quick, Ellie; we've got a lot on today!" Dan shouted after her.

Jess wondered just what they might have to do, but then reflected that Dan might have a meeting with his Probation Officer to discuss the forthcoming court case. She was not altogether surprised when later that morning a light tap was heard at the door and she opened it to find Ellie.

"Can I come in for a minute, Jess? Dan's gone to Berringden on the bus and won't be back until after lunch, he told me to stay with Mick, but he's disappeared somewhere, so I wondered if I could just wash a few things in the bathroom. I won't be long."

"That's fine, Ellie; would you like a hot drink?"

"Yes, a brew would be great. Milk and two sugars please."

Away from Dan, Ellie seemed a great deal more relaxed. She accepted the cup of tea Jess handed her and sat on the sofa.

"Ellie, you're in council care, so surely they have a duty to house you? It can't be much fun, this camping out in the middle of winter."

"Yea, they did offer me a place in the young people's hostel in Upper Berringden but they won't let Dan stay there, cos he's over eighteen."

"Couldn't you at least sleep there and see Dan during the day?"

Ellie shook her head. "Dan wouldn't allow it, I have to be with him. He was really cross with me for getting a shower at your place when he's not allowed one. He'd be mad if he knew I was here now."

"But you're an intelligent girl, so you must know that any man who really cared about his girlfriend wouldn't resent her taking a shower! I'm not sure that he can offer you much at the moment - a tent shared with an uncle in the cold. And what exactly are you all living on?"

"Dan signs on for the both of us as a couple so he gets a Giro, and I get £10 per week from my grandma. I go on the bus and meet her every Monday in Berringden. I'm not sure what Mick gets."

This was the first Jess had heard of any Ellie being in contact with any of her relatives. "Couldn't you stay with your Grandma, then? At least until the warmer weather comes."

"No, she did offer but I don't want to go cos she lives at Keighley and Dan can't stay there and I have to be with Dan! Besides, if my dad knew I was at my grandma's he'd come round and make trouble, then he'd go home and take it out on my mum and my little sister."

Jess was surprised to hear of a little sister, still living with allegedly unsatisfactory parents when Ellie had been taken into council care.

"Where are your family living, Ellie? How old is your sister?"

"Lower Berringden, my sister's eleven, but don't tell me to go back home, cos my dad abused me, that's why the council took me away."

"Of course I wouldn't tell you to return to an abusive father! But it puzzles me that the council think it safe to leave your sister there."

Ellie was beginning to sound agitated. "I dunno! Anyway, I have to go now, Dan'll be on the next bus." She put down her cup and began to collect her washing. Jess suggested that she leave the clothes to dry on the radiator, but Ellie shook her head.

"No, cos then he'll know I was here. I'll tell him I washed my things in the stream so he won't mind. I can dry them on a line he's put up in the trees near where we pitch the tent. I doubt anyone will steal them..."

Ellie gathered her things and quickly ran the few hundred yards down to the bus stop at the junction with the main road. She was just in time, since Dan was indeed getting off the bus. The more she found out about Ellie, the more Jess worried about her; she decided that she must take some sort of action, although she was not sure quite what to do. Getting in touch with the council was always problematic since it took such a long time to get past the call centre, one could be hanging on for an hour listening to endless brass band music. Jess had received no response to her email to the council, yet here was a young girl in their care, who had apparently escaped from an abusive family only to hitch up with a controlling boyfriend. Jess wondered how just best to proceed.

Chapter 18

Still unsure of the correct course of action, Jess decided to sleep on it. However, the following day brought a slew of messages into her email in-box, making for alarming reading. Word had got out that Jess was trying to help the rough sleepers, and various local people were warning her not to become further involved. She learned that Ellie had run away from the council-run hostel where there was a warden always present so she would have been safe. Dan was intentionally homeless after being bailed to his mother's house with a police monitoring tag, which he had somehow contrived to lose; he was therefore on the run, sleeping rough to avoid detection. As for the mysterious Uncle Mick, Jess read with alarm that he was a convicted paedophile hiding from supervision. Jess was now all the more determined to try to rescue young Ellie from these desperate circumstances, if indeed the girl would permit herself to be saved.

The tent was already in the shed when Jess went to fetch Izzy's lead, so it seemed the campers had made an early start. There was no sign of any of them all day until dusk brought a tap on the door and a tearful Ellie appeared. She explained that she and Dan had had a huge row, he had been mean to her ever since she had accepted Jess's invitation to take a shower, and had still not forgiven her. So now they had split up and she was waiting for her friend from Northfield on the other side of the village to come for her so she could stay with her. Would it be all right if she waited at Jess's house for her friend to arrive? Jess agreed, and made a cup of tea. Another knock on the door brought Ellie's friend, who introduced herself as Maya; Jess immediately recognised her as being the girl she had seen with Dan on the day Ellie had run past her in tears, heading for the railway line, some weeks previously. Ellie and Maya had a hurried *soto voce* conversation in the kitchen.

"Jess can we have some money for chips, please? The gas has been cut off at Maya 's so we can't cook anything. Dan's got all our money and food so I can't get anything from him. He claims benefit for us both as I'm too young to claim but he won't let me have any money."

"Oh dear, I don't think I have much cash in the house. Can't you borrow some from a friend at Northfield, Maya? Or get someone over there to cook you a meal? A relative maybe?"

"Oh, no, not really," said Maya. "My mum's next door but I doubt she's got any food in, and she never has any money..."

Jess wondered how on earth people lived, with no food, money or power. She usually paid for her groceries using her debit card, so was not in the habit of keeping money in the house, and she certainly did not want to lend the girls her bank card. However, a local farm which she passed on her walks sold eggs from a stall, with an honesty box for cash payment, for which Jess kept a small stash of coins. She looked in the kitchen table drawer, finding £3.10 in change in her egg money tin.

"This is all I have," said Jess, handing the coins to Ellie. The girls looked rather unimpressed, but Jess reminded them that this amount was sufficient to buy them some chips. Then she wondered if the 'no food, no money, no power' story was just a fabrication, and that they were really wanting money to buy drugs. Jess pondered whether she ought to offer to cook them a meal, but decided against it. She reminded herself that Ellie had the option of staying at the young peoples' hostel with a bed and use of the kitchen; she had chosen to live as she did, in the woods with a couple of criminals. Jess then made the mistake of mentioning the hostel and the possibility of Ellie returning there, now that she had split up with Dan.

"Don't be stupid!" snapped Ellie. " I can't go back there! Would you go back to somewhere you'd been raped? Come on Maya, let's go!"

Ellie made a run for the door while Maya shrugged at Jess, as if to say 'what can you do?' and followed Ellie down the road.

Jess was of course unaware that Ellie had been raped at the hostel. How had that happened, with a Warden always on the premises? The young girl's story seemed to be getting worse at every meeting with Jess, but at least she was now out of Dan's clutches and could perhaps begin to make better choices. She was still only sixteen so really ought to be in college.

After a fitful night's sleep, worrying about Ellie, Jess woke with a clear plan of action. She would telephone one of the local ward councillors, who had direct access to the various local authority departments without the hassle of going through the call centre. Jess knew the local ward representative Councillor Morag Bentley, having met her on a number of occasions at local fêtes and fairs, at one of which Morag had bought Jess's book. Cllr. Morag had also recently assisted Jess when she had been wrongfully accused of creating a noise nuisance. All the local Councillors' phone numbers were freely available for their constituents to contact them so Jess decided this is what she would now do. However, before she could take any action she heard the usual clattering in the yard, and saw to her dismay Dan with Ellie, making for the shed with their various items of bedding and luggage. There was no sign of Uncle Mick.

"Ellie, do you want to come in and use the bathroom?"

Ellie looked fearfully at Dan, who nodded grimly, telling her to be quick and he would wait. Once Ellie was inside Jess confronted her.

"I thought you two had split up! You said you were going to be staying with Maya!"

"Dan sussed out that I would be at Maya's and came round to get me, so I had to go with him, I've got no choice!"

"You have every choice! Listen, several people have got in touch with me, they're very worried about you, they claim that Uncle Mick is a paedophile and Dan's on the run from the police. Is this really how you want to live your life, Ellie?"

"Them's nasty rumours, none of that's right! People spread these stories cos they're spiteful, you really don't want to believe them." Ellie flounced out of the kitchen and returned to where Dan was waiting for her at the gate. She immediately reported what Jess had told her, and Dan threw Jess a withering glance through the window before marching back into the yard and retrieving the tent and all the bags from the shed.

"Time to move on. Sorry you believe all that wicked talk about me and Mick but we'd best go somewhere where folk aren't so gullible."

Jess felt relieved to see them go. She was about to report the situation to the authorities and she felt that this would be easier now that the trio's possessions were no longer stored in her shed. She opened her emails and checked the in-box, only to discover an alarming message from a local man named Simon, whom she did not know, but with whom it appeared she shared several mutual acquaintances.

"Dear Jess, I hear that you are helping Dan and Ellie and 'Uncle' Mick. I first met them in the autumn at the Drop-In centre I run at the church hall, they came in for free coffee and I got chatting to them. On learning that they were homeless I felt offered them the use of my holiday chalet in the woods above Upper Berringden for free over the Christmas period. It was fully equipped with bedding, kitchen utensils, plus TV and DVD player. I attach photographs of the state in which it was left on New Year's Day. You can see the space in the unit where the TV and DVD player used to be. They trashed the place, stole all the bedding and sold the electrical equipment in order to buy drugs. One picture shows their discarded cannabis sachets. To the best of my knowledge, Uncle Mick is a convicted paedophile, while Dan has an assault charge pending. Ellie is in complete thrall to Dan, she has a hostel place which she refuses to take up. She will tell you that her family abused her but the truth is that they disapproved of her relationship with Dan so she ran away to be with him. I trust you will think very carefully about what kind of assistance you continue to offer them in future. Yours, Simon."

Jess reached for the phone and dialled Councillor Bentley's number. Morag informed Jess that she had only just returned from holiday the previous evening and was still catching up with recent developments in the ward she represented. Jess said she hoped that she had had a good holiday, since a matter of some importance now required her urgent attention. A young girl in council care was living rough with a couple of questionable male companions. Jess outlined the story so far and asked Councillor Bentley to liaise with the appropriate authorities.

"You say they have left the playing field and taken all their things from your shed, so where do you think they might they be now?"

"I doubt they will be far away. I can ask around and let you know if I hear anything."

Just then there was a knock on the door. "Morag, could you hold on a minute, please? This might be them coming back for something!" Jess laid the phone receiver on the table and opened the door to reveal her neighbour, Damien, who had helped the trio with a donation of food.

"I've just had a call from Dan, he wants me to bring some food and cider to their new place, he says they're camping in the clog factory car park. I'm not sure whether to take them anything more though cos I've been hearing bad things about the uncle. That lass ought to be in care, not camping out with someone like him, in this weather..."

"Yes, I'm just trying to get some advice from Councillor Bentley." Jess returned to the phone. "Morag, are you still there? My neighbour tells me they're now camping behind the old clog factory."

Councillor Bentley promised to contact the Social Services department, and as good as her word, she rang back at teatime, with the news that the police had gone to the disused clog factory car park with a Place of Safety order and removed Ellie. The police confirmed that Uncle Mick was indeed a convicted paedophile, a fact of which Dan and Ellie had professed themselves unaware. The Councillor had asked about the allegation of rape at the council-run young people's hostel, and been assured that nothing of the sort had taken place on the premises, although it was possible that Ellie had been assaulted in the vicinity somewhere outside the hostel.

"She's safe now, then!" sighed Jess. However, Morag pointed out that since Ellie had not committed any offence there would be a 24 hour limit to the time that the Social Services could keep her, and if she wished to return to Dan there would be nothing they could do to prevent this.

The following day Councillor Bentley rang Jess again, with an update. Ellie had gone straight back to Dan, telling the social workers that she loved him and must be with him. The couple had made their way to Hebden Bridge, where there was a voluntary Drop-In centre offering free coffee, advice and support for people in difficulty. However, the centre manager there had reported that Uncle Mick was no longer with them.

"Well, that's good. There was something rather sinister about him. I don't see what more I could have done. Ellie has had the opportunity to break with Dan and return to college but that's clearly not what she wants, or at least, it's not what he'll let her do. He controls all their money and food, in fact, I think that maybe he just finds it useful to be able to claim an increase in his benefit for nominally supporting her. He certainly hasn't been treating her very well recently, so we can only hope that he takes better care of her from now on."

Chapter 19

The Berringden Brow Facebook page carried a short video from a man who said he was being evicted from his small-holding and was therefore offering free fruit tree cuttings to anyone who cared to collect them from his hilltop home. Jess set off to investigate, and discovered a lane along which she had never before been in all her years in the Berringden Valley. Passing through the remote hamlet of Pinfold, which Jess had always imagined to be a dead end, she found to her surprise a narrow cobbled road leading up towards the moor top. The man with the fruit bushes had mentioned in his film that his place was half a mile or so up this lane on the left, just before the road became a muddy track. Jess noticed a fenced garden a short distance across a field, although there was no sign of any dwelling. However, the road became muddy just a few yards ahead so this could only be the place. Jess went through the gate and into the field, skirting a small flock of sheep. A man waved at her from the garden.

"Are you the man with the fruit bushes?" asked Jess.

"Yes, I'm Andy. You saw the video? You're welcome to as many cuttings as you want, just help yourself. Here's some secateurs."

"Thanks, Andy." Jess began snipping at the blackcurrants. "I'm surprised you can grow fruit right up here. It's very exposed."

"Well, I had brushwood screens all round the orchard but the new landlord has taken them down. You see, the farmer who let me settle here twenty years ago has died and his heir wants me off the land. Me and the missus have been living off grid all this time, it's been great, but all good things come to an end so we're moving house – literally! We've found a bit of land in Cornwall, so we're going to have to dismantle the whole place and take it in pieces on a wagon."

Looking beyond a dry stone wall at the end of the orchard, Jess could see a ramshackle low wooden structure with a smoking chimney. It looked like something from a book of children's stories or nursery rhymes. A crooked little house with randomly placed windows down a crooked path. Jess almost expected to see a crooked cat saunter out. A besom beside the door completed the illusion of a fairy house.

"Yes, that's our humble abode. Would you like to look round? I've built it out of reclaimed bits and bats. I used to be roadie for the group Flat Caps and a Whippet, you may have heard of them, they were big in the 90s. So this bit here is from their stage set, and this wall is made of wood rescued after the Berringden Valley floods from a few years ago. I've added to it over the years; wood burner, this Belfast sink someone chucked out; lovely old doors – far too nice to waste! It's amazing what you can find in skips."

Jess was chiefly wondering about water and sanitary facilities.

"How do you manage for water and toilets? Spring water I suppose and a cess pit?"

"The farmer has piped water to fill the sheep troughs so I just extended the pipe to bring water into the house. And we've got compost toilets."

"It's going to be a job moving all this four hundred miles - just getting it out of the field and into the valley will be challenging, down that twisting cobbled lane. But it will be much warmer in Cornwall, you'll be able to grow a greater variety of fruit and veg."
"I've got a great gang ready and waiting to help and we're looking forward to it. But it seemed a pity to waste all the blackcurrants, the new landowner will simply uproot them. Are you sure you've got enough? Oh, I see a couple more people coming this way, with luck I'll soon get rid of most of the bushes. What about this medlar tree, do you think you could manage that if I dug it up for you? Such an unusual fruit, you have to leave them to almost go rotten, or 'blet' before you can cook them."

"I had a medlar tree when I lived near Selby. I made crumbles, but as you say the fruit is hard and you have to leave it for a good while. I'd love it, but I'm afraid I've nowhere to put it. Maybe your next visitors will have room for it."

Jess gave Andy a small donation towards the cost of the removal.

"Enough to buy the gang a big carton of milk for their brews when we're dismantling. It'll be thirsty work. Thanks very much, Jess!"

"I'm sorry I haven't much money with me. Good luck with the move and your new life in Cornwall!"

Jess sometimes wished she could move back to the warm West Country, but her house was built of Yorkshire stone and firmly rooted in Berringden Brow.

Chapter 20

Early February saw the traditional Celtic celebration of Imbolc in the nearby village of Marsden. This coincides with the Christian festival of St. Brigid, the fire and fertility saint, and falls midway between the winter solstice and the Spring equinox. Jess and Zofia drove over the hills to Marsden and joined the procession wending its way to the field where various entertainments centred on fire were to take place. Dramatic fire jugglers, fire dancers and flame swallowers entertained the crowds, and finally the giant silvery winter frost man struggled with his towering green counterpart; naturally, the Green man won, since Spring was inexorably on the way.

By the middle of the month, Jess was longing for signs of the long-promised Spring. The winter had been very wet, and she was becoming tired of wading along muddy paths on her daily walks with Izzy. The dog was equally fed up, and often dug her paws in, refusing to budge if she thought the day was too wet or icy. Nick frequently arrived home drenched, having forgotten to take a hat or umbrella with him on his rounds. Jess wondered if a snowdrop walk might cheer them up. She had been following the progress of the lengthy renovations at Wentworth Woodhouse for some time; this had once been the largest private house in England but had fallen into disrepair and was being restored with the aid of lottery money. Jess had picked up a book about the history of the house, *Black Diamonds*, by Catherine Bailey, at the solicitor's office when she went to make her Will. The solicitor was running late so Jess had been obliged to wait for her appointment and needed something to read. The receptionist said someone had left the book behind, and that Jess could have it.

It turned out that Wentworth Woodhouse had a fascinating history, involving a possible Canadian changeling child, a royal visit by King George and Queen Mary and a scandalous and tragic connection with the Kennedy family, so after reading it, Jess had started to follow the house's Facebook page. There was an on-going programme of events to raise additional money for the huge repair bill. Jess and Nick had previously been on a tour of the house, culminating with tea in the Long Gallery, and had on a separate occasion undertaken a rooftop tour, donning hard hats and climbing up a temporary outside staircase to look down on the site where thousands of tiles were being replaced and ornaments restored. They had not yet seen the gardens, presently carpeted with snowdrops, so Jess bought tickets. She arranged for Izzy to spend the afternoon with Frank, which meant a slight detour to his house in order to drop her off. Jess thought she would be very clever and cut across country to reach Wentworth Woodhouse, rather than returning to the motorway, using an old Ordnance Survey map of the area. She instructed Nick to call out the various turnings as they came to them. However, map-reading was not Nick's forte, and they ended up going a long way round through various villages. The snowdrop walk was scheduled for 2pm and Jess was by now beginning to think they would be late, despite having allowed what she had hoped was plenty of time. On their previous visits to Wentworth Woodhouse they had arrived from the M1, and since they were now approaching from a completely different direction, nothing looked familiar. The map did not seem to bear much resemblance to the actual road lay-out on the ground, and Jess wondered if the roads had been altered since it was published. They had come past a roundabout which was definitely not marked. She parked the car in a lay-by and tried to get instructions from her phone, but the signal was poor. Next, she knocked on a few nearby cottage doors to see if she could get proper directions, but no-one was at home. She then flagged down a passing cyclist, but he was not sure where the house was. Finally, she found a man in a garden, who told her to go into the village and turn right at the war memorial. The house would then be a short distance on the left.

Jess and Nick drove deep into the countryside, having done as the man had told them, but there was no sign of the house. They turned off the road into a new housing estate where Jess frantically knocked on several doors until she found a helpful woman who told her she should actually have turned left at the war memorial. Her previous adviser had apparently not known right from left. Jess hastily turned the car round and sped back towards the village, obeying the helpful woman's instructions but disregarding all speed limits, and arrived at Wentworth Woodhouse a minute before 2 o'clock. Rushing up the path to the front entrance in a dishevelled state, she discovered to her relief that the 2pm walk had been postponed for a quarter of an hour in order for the guide to return from his lunch. Usually there were several volunteer guides available but today it seemed many had gone down with colds so that one man was having to escort all the snowdrop tours...Meanwhile, Nick, who disliked rushing anywhere, had sauntered up to the front door. Jess explained the situation and said that at least they would now have time for a cup of tea and a trip to the loo before the tour. They drank their tea quickly and returned to the main entrance, only to find that their snowdrop walk had already left.

"But we were told it was delayed by a quarter of an hour!"

The official on the door said that that had indeed been the original plan, but that Neil, the lone available guide, had hurried back quickly after lunch so as not to keep the 2pm walkers waiting long.

"Don't worry, we'll find them!" said the official, escorting Jess and Nick to a side door. "They'll probably be up this way!"

The woman ran to the top of an incline, followed by Jess and Nick, sliding on the muddy path. Jess was glad she was wearing stout shoes and had brought her walking pole. At the top of the slope they could see a few bedraggled snowdrops, but there was no sign of the official tour.

"They must have gone down here," said their impromptu guide, dashing along another track, skirting a huge stone statue of a naked god, looking rather forlorn in the wind and rain. After several twists and turns, they finally came upon the snowdrop party. Neil the guide was surprised at the sight of latecomers, having been assured that everyone was present.

Neil turned out to be an excellent guide, explaining how the gardens had been dug up by order of Emmanuel Shinwell in order to mine the coal beneath. The house was at the time being used as a Women's Training College and the Principal had insisted that the front lawn be protected in order that her girls might have somewhere to practice netball. However, there remained a large spoil heap in the middle of the grounds, which was still unsafe even after all these years. Shinwell had resented the aristocracy and their splendid houses, so the destruction of the gardens was judged to have been ordered out of spite. Jess noticed a number of pheasants, and Neil commented that they sought safety in the grounds from the surrounding shoots. "They're wise enough to know they're safe here; when the beaters come through to drive them out, the birds simply fly straight back."

Jess was pleased to hear it. They made their way along the path, passing a huge three-hundred-year old tree, to where a padlocked gate indicated the present extent of the grounds. Beyond was a commercial garden centre, in what had been the kitchen garden of the house. Neil explained that Wentworth Woodhouse had actually grown its own pineapples in the days when these were not eaten but were prized as dinner-table centrepieces because of their rarity value. The old Duke of Devonshire had come specially from Chatsworth in order to discover the secret of pineapple cultivation in the North of England. It had actually been possible to rent a pineapple to impress one's house party guests, and return it afterwards. However, the fruit did not last indefinitely and would eventually succumb to maggots, so it was important to select a specimen robust enough to withstand a long journey and preferably one which had not been previously borrowed too many times. A hostess did not want this prized fruit and useful talking point to disintegrate onto the best table linen and to have maggots wriggling around fine dining china and silver cutlery, alarming her guests and putting them off their banquet.

Jess had expected carpets of snowdrops, and in this respect the gardens were disappointing, with intermittent clumps dotted about. Neil observed that they were a work in progress, with volunteers daily planting more bulbs. There were a number of rhododendrons in bloom, fairly unusual for February, and daffodils about to come out, so what with the pheasants and statues the gardens were not without interest. Jess and Nick thanked Neil and returned to the car park.

They made their way back to Frank's house to collect Izzy via the motorway route, avoiding the villages. Jess was disappointed to see that the stair carpet she had given Frank was looking quite shabby. He had evidently not attempted to clean it since Jess and Nick's last visit, despite the fact that his Hoover was now working. Jess then wondered if she should set to and clean it herself, but she simply hadn't the heart. She had hoped that improving Frank's life in one small way, with the gift of a decent stair carpet, would lift his spirits a little and give him an incentive to do a bit more housework, but this had proved not to be the case. Jess recalled her previous attempts to help friends, which had frequently backfired and were often actually resented, since those living with depression and other mental health problems may not welcome any interference, however well intentioned. Jess recalled being screamed at by a friend, Anne, living with bi-polar disorder when Anne had accused her of not doing enough to help her, of not visiting often enough nor staying for sufficient time, and of failing to prevent her from falling into the clutches of a con woman posing as an expert de-clutterer. Anne lived in London and Jess could not afford to visit often, but she had attended many care planning meetings and visited when Anne was hospitalised under a Section of the Mental Health Act. There was a limit to what a well-meaning friend could achieve in such situations.

At least Izzy did not mind the state of Frank's house - she had had a pleasant afternoon, enjoying a walk up the lane to visit a field with some horses, returning for a snooze on Frank's sofa, followed by tea. Jess reflected that everyone has different standards so she must try not be judgmental; after all, her own house, while tidy enough, was not exactly pristine. However, she was concerned for Frank's health. His constant coughing and sneezing was unlikely to be ameliorated while he was still surrounded by so much dust and grime, to which he was allergic. But as Tom later pointed out, if Frank himself was unconcerned about the state of his house why ever should she worry?

Chapter 21

It seemed to Jess that she had been listening to *The Archers* all her life. Her mother had been a devotee of the radio soap opera, so Jess had begun listening involuntarily and over the years had became hooked. Apart from the period spent in Botswana, beyond the reach of Radio 4 she had maintained the habit of listening over many years. *The Archers* had begun broadcasting in the year of her birth and Jess had found that she was the same age as Eddie Grundy, give or take a couple of days. So when Jess discovered that a Facebook group of Archers fans was planning a conference, she decided to attend.

The conference was to be held at a Southern university, and the papers to be presented bore quasi-academic titles, involving such subjects as kinship networks and economic structures within the village of Ambridge and the county of Borsetshire. There was also to be a presentation about local drainage systems and the disastrous Ambridge floods which had resulted in the death of the silent but oft-referred to character, Freda Fry. A number of well-regarded academics were involved in organising the event, and there was the promise of an appearance by one of the cast's leading lights. Some people commented that they would find this rather disconcerting, in that actors in the flesh never looked anything like the listeners' idea of the character they were portraying; while other die-hard fans stated flatly that they would boycott any proceedings involving so-called actors because of course everyone knew *The Archers* was real.

As usual, Nick was happy to look after Izzy for the weekend, so Jess set off for the station. The train was crowded and Jess was glad she had booked a seat. She was engrossed in her Sudoku when the man sitting next to her leaned over and pointed to her half-solved puzzle.

"You're cheating!" he announced in a loud voice,.

"No, I'm not!" said Jess, hoping he would mind his own business.

"Yes, you **are** cheating; you can't put two figures in the squares."

One of Jess's methods when solving Sudoku was to write the only two possible numbers in a square, so that if she found another square where the same two numbers were the only possible solutions she could then safely eliminate those two numbers as being correct anywhere else. Everyone has their own method of puzzle-solving, and Jess's worked for her.

By now, half the carriage was listening intently, as the objectionable man ranted on about Jess's Sudoku misdemeanours. People looked up from newspapers, paused mid-sandwich or told their children to hush while they listened to this intriguing tirade. Even the ticket inspector halted his inspecting, and stood patiently beside the angry man, awaiting the outcome of the Sudoku contretemps before asking to check his ticket.

"It's a perfectly valid method of solving a Sudoku puzzle," said the exasperated Jess, annoyed at having to justify herself and also that there was not a spare seat in the carriage to which she could move.

"No, it's not; it's cheating!" The awful man was determined not to let the matter go. By now, the surrounding passengers were engaged in a heated debate as to the best way of solving a Sudoku, with the ticket inspector actually claiming to have a quick and foolproof method. Jess reached for her suitcase and gathered up her belongings. She decided that sitting on the floor outside the carriage would be better than having to put up with the dreadful man in the next seat. A young man on the opposite side of the gangway smiled sympathetically at her and offered to swap seats. He was merely reading a book, rather than being engaged in controversial puzzle solving, so should be safe from the attentions of the oafish fellow passenger. Jess nodded gratefully, but at that moment the guard announced that the train was pulling into Sheffield and Jess's Sudoku critic rose from his seat, scowled at Jess and made for the door. As he left the carriage, Jess thankfully resumed her place and tried to settled back to her puzzle. However, she found that she was still so annoyed that she was not in the mood to finish it, and was reduced to idly glancing at the newspaper's gossip column instead, looking at pictures of 'celebrities' of whom she had never heard. She recalled Alex's advice that the best way of dealing with many people was simply to tell them to 'f... off', and Jess often wished that she had had the courage to try this; however, there were children present in the carriage and she had no wish to offend anyone or draw any more attention to herself.

Jess reached her destination without further incident and took a bus to the budget hotel where she had booked for two nights. She quickly changed and then set off for the Museum of Farming and Rural Life which was hosting the conference opening event, a presentation about recent technological developments in farming, followed by a buffet supper and a chance to look around the many exhibits. These illustrated farming practices and rural ways of life of yesteryear. Jess was aware that this was where Edwin had spent his career, since he had been for thirty years the librarian at this very museum before taking early retirement a decade ago.

Jess had always enjoyed spending the occasional afternoon in a Pick Your Own strawberry field, but realised that she would not care to do this full-time. Nor would many other British people, it seemed, and, with the supply of European fruit pickers now likely to diminish, the young man giving the opening presentation declared that robots were the way forward. Prototypes were being developed, with speed and accuracy improving all the time, as *Archers* listeners were of course already aware, from hearing about engineer Alice Aldridge's work in this area, so that fruit and vegetable crops need not rot in the fields for want of pickers. Jess was relieved to hear it.

The vegetarian supper was delicious, and provided an opportunity to chat with other *Archers* fans. The opening question was usually 'How long have you been listening?' to which Jess could truthfully reply that she had listened almost continuously since the programme's inception, even while in her mother's womb. Jess then set off to look around the many galleries; there were really far too many exhibits to properly take in during one brief visit, as the staff wanted everyone out by eight o'clock; however, Jess was determined to discover what *Archers* related items the museum might possess. She was pleased to find a selection of books, pottery and a few jigsaws, since the BBC had licensed a considerable amount of *Archers* merchandise over the programme's long history. Zofia had given Jess a set of Jennifer Aldridge's cookbooks, discovered in a charity shop, for Christmas, although Jess had not yet actually got around to cooking any of the recipes, most of which seemed rather extravagant when compared with Jess's frugal methods of domestic management. Of course, Jennifer was married to a landed gentleman farmer, so luxury ingredients such as game birds and venison were readily available. The one *Archers* recipe that Jess had so far attempted she had found in another book, relating the early history of the family. It was for Sussex Pond Pudding, a concoction of suet pastry, grated butter, demerara sugar and a lemon, which was said to have been a favourite dish of Phil Archer. She had posted a picture of the result on Facebook, and this had caused general hilarity among her friends, with comments such as "Are you sure you followed the recipe properly, Jess?" and "Whatever is that yellow thing in the middle?" The 'thing' was of course the whole lemon, pierced thoroughly in order to release the juice during cooking, as stated in the recipe, which Jess had in fact carefully followed; although admittedly, the resulting dish did look rather odd. However, Nick had pronounced it delicious and a nice change from crumble, and another supportive friend had actually asked Jess for the recipe.

The next day's sessions were mostly light-hearted, comparing *The Archers* with TV family *The Simpsons,* examining the viability of a goat yoga business, and a discussion about the rival matriarchs of Ambridge. However, on a much more serious note, a recent long-running storyline involving domestic abuse within marriage, where perpetrator Rob Titchenor had used physical force and mental cruelty over a prolonged period to subjugate his wife Helen, was praised for its effect in encouraging other abused people to come forward to ask for help. Titchenor had isolated Helen from her family and friends, dictating which clothes she should wear and continually 'gas-lighting' her; his behaviour reminded Jess of her father, Jack, who had used belittling and demeaning tactics with her mother, half a century previously. He had continually beaten her, and had grudgingly given her the housekeeping allowance on a 'payment by results' system, supposedly adjusted according to the cleanliness of the house and his opinion of the meals that week, but in reality reduced according to his whim. He never hesitated to withhold ten precious shillings if he considered that things were not up to scratch on the domestic front but kept the money himself to buy drink He continually criticised his wife's cooking, and Jess's too, insisting that he required pastry that 'melted in the mouth' and refusing to eat meals not up to his exacting gastronomic standards, declaring that as an Epicure with an educated palate he was offended by the indifferent culinary offerings of his anxious wife and terrified daughter.

Considering education completely unnecessary for a girl, he had turned Jess out of the house when she was trying to revise for exams, so that she had been obliged to study in nearby fields or seek shelter with sympathetic neighbours. Now fifty years later, this cruel behaviour had been made unlawful, although of course Jack had acted with impunity in the 1960s, when a man was master in his own home and all other family members were subjugated to his will. Not even the Police could intervene between husband and wife, children were regarded as the property of their parents, and there were no helplines or refuges. Today, the conference audience applauded the writing team of *The Archers* for tackling and bringing to light the previously hidden topic of coercive control.

Back in Berringden Brow, Zofia presented Jess with a decorated pebble as a Mothering Sunday gift. Jess murmured her thanks, and Zofia went on the explain that the pebble was an orgonite. Jess had never heard of orgonites and had no idea what they were used for, so Zofia explained that orgone was a substance which drew in negative energy and transmuted it into positive energy, a spiritual healing tool. A colleague of hers made the orgonites and they were currently becoming popular, having been recently rediscovered, after the Beat generation artists and poets had used them in the 1950s as part of the counterculture movement. Jess thanked Zofia and placed the object on her desk; she hoped the orgonite would work, although she could not help but feel a little sceptical.

Chapter 22

Zofia announced that she was going for a Gong Bath on her day off, and asked whether Jess would like to accompany her. Jess was unsure as to what exactly a Gong Bath entailed. Zofia explained that no water was involved, it was simply necessary for participants to lie on a mat and relax while listening to the soothing sounds as the leader struck various gongs. During a gong bath, listeners typically experienced a sense of connectedness and peace while the gong sounds could be helpful in rebalancing the body, physically, emotionally and spiritually. Jess was rather reluctant to commit the £5 charge, fearing that Gong Baths might not suit her, until she found out that the initial session would be a free taster, in order that she could determine whether gong bathing was indeed for her. Zofia told her that it was advisable to bring one's own mat to lie on, although it was possible to sit in a comfy chair if someone had difficulty getting down on the floor, or once down, found it hard to get up again.

As was quite usual at a Hebden Bridge event, the room smelled of incense and a CD of ambient noise was playing softly as people were welcomed into the room. Jess found a space to unroll her camping mat, while beside her Zofia was using her yoga mat. On the other side of Jess was a large woman lying on a fleece blanket, and next to her was someone using an old coat. A few older women and a couple of elderly men were sitting around the edge of the room on chairs. The group leader, Aleida, had erected a sturdy frame from which was suspended an array of large gongs, and there was an assortment of other percussion instruments laid out in front of the frame. Jess recognised a wooden tube containing seeds, used to imitate the sound of soft rain, from her long-ago primary school music lesson days.

The session began, but Jess found it difficult to relax and benefit from the soothing sounds. She was reminded of the time she and her friend Stella had attended a meditation session at the local Buddhist monastery one stormy evening. Stella had succeeded in meditating but Jess was all too aware of the wind blowing tree branches against the window pane, making an urgent tapping sound as though someone was asking to be let in, rather as in *Wuthering Heights*. She always found it difficult to detach herself from her surroundings, and today she could hear traffic passing by on the nearby street, and the clattering of crockery from an adjacent room where evidently tea was being brewed for another group. Elsewhere, a workman was inconsiderately whistling and using an electric drill. Then a sudden burst of heavy rain pattered against the window, drowning out the soft sound of the rain imitating percussion instrument. To further add to the cacophony the woman next to Jess had a rumbling stomach, audible even above the sound of the gongs and other ambient noise. Jess was glad she had not been required to pay the fee, but glancing surreptitiously across at Zofia, she was pleased to see that her daughter-in-law seemed to be deeply relaxed and was evidently getting her money's worth. Afterwards, Jess thanked Aleida for the opportunity to participate in the session; but she later confided to Zofia that she did not feel gong-bathing was really her cup of tea.

The Film Club showing that month was *Grow Your Own* a comedy concerning a group of city allotment holders who resent the fact that a number of refugees are about to be given plots. However, as the locals get to know the new arrivals, they come to appreciate that they not only have good knowledge of the range of exotic vegetables that can be grown in England, but also that several of them have very useful skills, notably a doctor who qualified overseas but who is not yet permitted to practice in the UK. This man's garden shed becomes an informal consulting room, with the locals bringing him a range of ailments, and they are deeply concerned when news comes that the doctor and his family might be deported. One young man develops a crush on a refugee woman, to the annoyance of a local lady who has a crush on **him.** The point is gently made that the general population will enjoy the company of newcomers once they get to know them. Jess told Ben that she thought this was an interesting choice of film.

Jess's next engagement was a supper talk to a group of elderly Bradford Methodists who met monthly for a shared meal. Jess was never very keen to speak at any event where food was involved, since it often seemed that her audience would really prefer to put their heads down on the tables and snooze after the meal, rather than listen to her. Many an elderly person had nodded off during one of her lunchtime talks, in fact an address to one Darby and Joan group of nonagenarians on a warm summer day following a good lunch had resulted in almost the entire audience snoring. Jess herself had found it hard to concentrate on her talk and only the slightly younger co-ordinator managed to stay awake to laugh at Jess's jokes. On this occasion the Bradford Methodists were enjoying a cold buffet, and Jess was shown to a table with five other people, all tucking in to quiche, mini sausage rolls, sandwiches and salad. Conversation was practically non-existent since everyone was busily engaged in the serious business of eating supper, until it was time for the cups of tea to be served, when people relaxed and began chatting. The standard enquiry of Jess was "Where have you come from?" Frequently the questioner had not heard of Berringden Brow, so Jess usually added that it was not far from Hebden Bridge, of which most audiences were aware, nodding sagely with comments such as "Ah, the hippies!" or "Lots of tourists but nowhere to park..." Jess sometimes felt constrained to add that she was in fact originally from Devonshire, in order to forestall the frequently voiced follow-up comment, "Well, tha' doesn't sound like tha's from round 'ere, lass!"

Today, the elderly gentleman sitting to Jess's right took up the theme of origins and announced that he was from St. Kitts and had arrived more than seventy years ago on the MV *Empire Windrush* in answer to the call for people from the British Empire to work in the textile mills and other manufacturing occupations. His wife, who was sitting next to him stirring sugar into his teacup, had later joined him and they had lived in Bradford ever since. Over the years they had made several trips back home, but sadly they were now too old and infirm to undertake the journey. It had been hard at first in the post-war climate, but Bradford had later become so very multicultural that they now felt completely at home.

The helpers began to clear away the crockery and cutlery and a young man arrived to fold away and stack the tables. Everyone was encouraged to move to a comfortable chair, walking frames were stowed and tea trolleys wheeled away. Jess was introduced and began her talk by recounting an incident which had occurred on a train, when an elderly lady had accosted her, a complete stranger, and insisted on recounting chapter and verse of her lengthy romantic history. Jess pointed out that younger people frequently isolated themselves on public transport by using ear phones plugged into their mobiles, so that Jess, who had been quietly absorbed in a crossword puzzle at the time, was seemingly the nearest available pair of open ears. Jess liked to make her talks interactive, and invited audience members to tell of any odd or unexpected encounters they might be happy to share with the group, before moving on to her next subject, which was funny incidents involving pets. Quite a few people responded and the variety this brought to the session made it all the more enjoyable for the audience than simply having to listen to the same voice for three quarters of an hour. Jess hoped that perhaps the Caribbean gentleman would contribute something interesting from his *Windrush* journey or subsequent trips, but although apparently attentive, he remained courteously silent. Meanwhile his wife was occupied with some oddly-shaped and colourful knitting, which spilled from her needles across her lap, covering her legs and reaching almost onto the floor. Jess was discreetly trying to discern what manner of garment this might possibly become, but could reach no firm conclusion.

At the end, the co-ordinator thanked Jess, asking her if she would be prepared to come again another time with a different selection of anecdotes. Jess said that she would be delighted to, since several people had already approached her saying how much they had enjoyed her talk. The co-ordinator then pressed a greaseproof paper parcel of left-over quiche and a few sandwiches into Jess's hand, saying that it would be a shame for the food to go to waste. The lady from St. Kitts gathered up her mysterious knitting into a huge multi-coloured bundle and deftly stowed it into a laundry bag which she handed to her husband to carry. The minibuses were about to convey the infirm members back home, walking frames were readied, coats and hats donned, and final goodbyes said. Jess could scarcely remember when she had enjoyed an evening as much.

Chapter 23

Jess and Izzy were returning from one of their walks with a large carrier bag of sweet docks, *Bistortum polygonum,* an early Spring plant which grew in profusion in the Berringden valley and which was used for making the local delicacy Dock Pudding. The World Dock Pudding Championships were held annually at the Community centre and always attracted a large crowd. As well as people cooking on the stage, there was always a brass band in attendance providing entertainment, plus various craft stalls around the room. Jess had never won the competition with her dock pudding, nor did she expect to, since she was of course not a native of the locality. Several successful competitors claimed to have secret family recipes which had been passed down the generations, while Jess had access only to the basic recipe of docks, nettles, Spring onions and oatmeal. The greens must be picked very early in the season, when they first emerged and before they became too stringy. Full of fortifying vitamins and minerals, in previous years the dish was regarded as a Spring tonic after the privations of winter.

Jess had collected her sweet docks along the cycle path, where they would not suffer from roadside pollution. She had also gathered a quantity of nettle heads, using gardening gloves to pick them. Upon cooking, the nettles' sting was neutralised so they were safe to eat. Jess was pleased that she had harvested such a large amount, since once cooked the volume of the wild greens diminished considerably.

"Hello Izzy!" A voice rang out and Jess saw Dan, the troubled young man she had tried to help at New Year, emerge from the nearby car park carrying a large shopping bag. He put the bag down on the wall and bent to pat Izzy, who always welcomed male attention and was joyfully wagging her tail. Jess recalled that her last encounter with Dan had been when he removed his tent and belongings from her shed, before she had contacted Councillor Morag Bentley about his girlfriend, Ellie. She wondered whether Dan would refer to this incident, and accuse her of interfering. She was therefore surprised when Dan finished patting Izzy and turned to face her, all smiles.

"I want to thank you, Jess, for what you did, contacting the police."

"It wasn't me who rang the police, Dan; I only got in touch with our local councillor because I was so concerned about Ellie sharing a tent with an alleged paedophile..."

"Well, you set the ball rolling, and when the police came and told us about Uncle Mick we was astonished cos we didn't honestly know about his shady past. We thought it was just malicious rumours. It came as a shock to us, I can tell you, and Ellie let rip, she gave him such a tongue lashing. The police took her away and gave me twenty-four hours to get rid of Mick before they would let her return. He's in Lower Berringden somewhere, but he's a dead man walking cos no-one wants to have nothing to do with him any more."

"Where are you living now? And what about Ellie?"

"We've got given a house now in Upper Berringden, me and Ellie, we're still together and everything's great."

"And how about your court case, how did that turn out?"

"Oh, the judge let me off with a twelve month community order. So as long as I behave myself there's nothing to worry about."

"Well, you'd better go straight now, you've too much to lose what with the house, and Ellie of course."

"I will Jess, I will: oh, and here's me friend arrived, gotta go now."

A car pulled up and Dan jumped into the back seat, which surprised Jess. Then she thought that maybe it was a minicab. She was about to leave when she noticed Dan's shopping bag still on the wall.

She picked it up and ran towards the car, which still had its engine running, shouting and waving.

"Dan, you've forgotten your shopping!"

Dan simply smiled and motioned her away. Jess could not understand why he should leave his bread, milk and beer cans behind on the wall. She approached the car. The driver wound down the front window and smiled.

"He says it's OK, he'll be going home in a minute."

The penny then dropped. Dan was not driving off in a minicab but had simply got into the back seat of a drug dealer's car in order to buy cannabis. He would no doubt be leaving when the deal was complete. Meanwhile Jess, with her shouting and waving, was unwittingly drawing attention to the transaction. She replaced Dan's shopping bag on the wall and left, feeling very foolish.

Chapter 24

The World Dock Pudding Championships were considered by many to be the highlight of the village calendar. Jess generally had a stall at the accompanying craft fair, selling her books, and this year she had decided to also take part in the cooking competition. It was a good year for the sweet docks, and of course, nettles, the other main ingredient, grew everywhere in profusion. Jess was always amazed to see how the greens dramatically decreased in volume during the cooking process, rather like spinach. Oatmeal and spring onions added bulk. The dish was traditionally served accompanying a fried breakfast. It was necessary to bring a frying pan, cooking implements and breakfast items as well as the actual dock pudding ingredients, so after carefully packing her basket and leaving Nick in charge of Izzy for a few hours, Jess set off for the Community centre. Dogs were permitted inside the main hall, but Izzy detested the sound of brass bands and always howled in protest whenever she heard a Sousa march, 'Finlandia' or the 'Going Home' theme from the New World Symphony, so Jess hdecided that it was safer to leave her with Nick.

There was added excitement this year since the event was being filmed by a television company. This was because the judging panel was set to comprise a couple of well-known comedians who lived locally, plus the Yorkshire TV weatherman. There was a posse of TV cameras following the comedians for a spoof documentary about their lives, and all competitors were asked if they would agree to being filmed. The residents of the Berringden Valley were by now very used to the presence of television cameras, since TV location managers seemed to love the Pennine scenery; *Last Tango in Halifax*, *Gentleman Jack* and *Happy Valley* were among the notable series filmed locally. Alex had also featured in a documentary film shot some years ago, entitled *Shed Your Tears and Walk Away,* about addiction in Hebden Bridge. Alex's comic cameo had provided one of the very few light-hearted moments of this sobering feature. Jess herself had almost appeared in the feature film *Walk Like a Panther* when she had accidentally stumbled onto an outdoor location on her way to a Methodist Chapel to give a talk to the local WI. A steward in high-viz jacket had stopped her in her tracks and directed her the long way round the village, along cobbled lanes and across a footbridge, to reach the chapel rather later than planned; however, the WI members had been very understanding.

Jess was on stage cooking her docks on a gas ring when she found herself under close scrutiny from the photographer sent by the local paper, the *Berringden Bugle,* who, not to be outdone by the TV crew, was also in attendance – indeed, his camera was almost in her frying pan and she feared that some of the bacon fat used to finish the dish might spurt onto the lens and obscure the picture. Meanwhile, the Hebden Bridge Junior Band played a selection of well-known tunes, and the craft stalls, arranged round the edge of the room, were in full swing. Jess had been obliged to leave her book stall unattended during the time she was on stage cooking; on a previous occasion she had enlisted the help of Frank, but she quickly discovered that he was no great salesman, sitting behind the stall looking exceedingly glum and in all likelihood deterring rather than attracting potential customers, Jess felt. She herself always smiled and tried to catch the eye of passers-by, inviting them to look at the books, explaining that they were entertaining, set locally and appealed especially to women of a certain age. With couples, Jess had developed a winning line of patter, "Sir, you'll be in her good books if you buy her one of mine!" which she found often worked well. The women giggled, while the men generally grinned and fished the money from their pockets.

Finally, all the contestants' dock puddings had been sampled by the judges behind closed doors, and the competitors were asked to assemble in front of the stage for the results. One of the comedians came forward to announce the winners and present the prizes. He began by declaring that no-one had actually been poisoned, which was a great relief. Jess was worried that someone might have cooked coarse docks by mistake rather than the sweet variety which the recipe required, thus laying low a couple of comedians and the weatherman. As she had anticipated, Jess did not win a prize, but she was happy simply to have taken part and to have supported a unique village event. Her stall had done well, with several books sold, so she collected up the remaining stock, plus her cooking equipment, and went home happy.

The following week, Jess was surprised to find a lovely picture of herself featured in the Berringden Bugle; evidently the photograph had not been spoiled by bacon fat. The villagers had to wait for some months until the television series following the lives of the comedian couple was shown, and Jess glimpsed herself in the line-up of dock pudding competitors. There was also a brief shot of her book stall. Of course the main emphasis of the programme was on the comedy couple attending a unique event in their quirky village.

Jess had donated a spare dock pudding to a fellow member of her choir, a Yorkshire woman who relished the dish, since Jess herself had found that she really did not care much for it. She put this down to being a Devonian. Recently, Alex and Zofia had developed a penchant for collecting wild foods, mainly of the fungal variety. Foraging was in the family, it seemed. Jess had once given Alex a copy of Richard Mabey's classic *Food For Free,* and he was using this to identify various food stuffs growing in local woods. Jess was anxious that he might one day pick a deadly poisonous fungus by mistake, but Alex assured her that he knew what he was doing.

Meanwhile, Zofia had created a delicious wild garlic pesto from the Ransoms plants which grew abundantly in local woodland, and Alex was impatiently waiting for the appearance of elderflowers to use for wine and cordial. Jess sometimes made a slightly alcoholic, fizzy elderflower drink, known in the West Country as Haymakers' Champagne, using a recipe given to her by her late godmother who had been a wise woman. Some years previously, the European Union had actually issued a proclamation banning the use of the word 'champagne' for any drink not emanating from that specific region of France; however, Jess had taken no notice of this particular directive, nor indeed any other, so far as she was aware, and still used the old name for the delicious fizzy concoction. She also sold home-made blackberry jam from her front garden every autumn, without a licence or the necessity of having had her kitchen inspected by bureaucrats. Jess recalled how years ago there had been an outcry about this particular directive, resulting in a special exemption for WI markets, so as a WI member, Jess felt that she should therefore be covered. Thankfully, she had yet to be reported to the authorities.

Alex informed her that he would also be dining off wild food, since his friend Kenny was making squirrel curry. Kenny was so fed up with the squirrels raiding his bird feeder that he had shot them.

"He's marinated them in lime juice and spices, should be delicious!"

Jess shuddered, since her interest in wild food did not extend as far as consuming rodents but was confined to the more unadventurous vegetarian items. Alex remarked that if the climate change scientists and soil experts were correct, with the world heating up and soil becoming degraded to the extent that there would soon be widespread famine, then foods such as squirrel meat, wild garlic pesto and dock pudding would become more widely acceptable, and foraging would be a necessity rather than merely a hobby; so that he, Zofia and Kenny were simply in the vanguard of what would eventually become a generally accepted method of obtaining food.

Chapter 25

The invitation to speak at the forthcoming Tiverton Grammar School alumni reunion had come as a pleasant surprise to Jess. The previous year had been the final opportunity for former pupils to view the lovely old Edwardian brick building before it was demolished to create a car-park for the new, quite unremarkable glass and steel structure which now formed the adjacent primary school. Of course, the Grammar School had been abolished in the 1970s, amalgamating with the Secondary Modern to form a Comprehensive. Items from the old school's archives had been on display the previous year - magazines, programmes from school plays, cuttings from the local paper regarding pupil exchange visits to France and Germany, hockey, cricket and rugby team photographs and various pieces of memorabilia. Jess had donated a copy of her book which included several chapters concerning school life in the 1960s. She had not imagined that anyone would actually take the trouble to read it, so it was with astonishment that she learned that one of the organisers of the reunion had actually done so and decided that she should be invited to be the guest speaker this year.

Jess and Izzy drove to Devon through the glorious Spring weather and reached their dog-friendly thatched farmhouse B and B at tea-time. Jess had decided that rather than trust the somewhat unreliable campervan she would borrow Nick's car and stay in comparative luxury on this occasion; her brother Jeff, who still lived in Devon, had told her that he would be away that weekend, so would be unable to accommodate her or to attend the reunion. Mrs. Bray, the farmer's wife and proprietor of the Bed and Breakfast part of the business, welcomed Jess and showed her to her room, which looked out over the cobbled farmyard complete with duck pond and cow byre. Beyond was field of lush grass with a flock of sheep contentedly grazing. The farm was set in a hollow, with no modern structures visible, although over the brow of the hill and safely out of sight there was a motorway and a wind farm. Jess thought it resembled a scene from a Thomas Hardy novel and would not have been the least bit surprised to discover that there was a milkmaid named Tess.

However, the bucolic illusion was quickly shattered when the farmer arrived on a noisy quad bike, with a collie dog sitting behind him barking furiously.

The organisers of the reunion had previously contacted Jess to explain that there would not be as many former pupils as usual attending this year's event, in fact they could not have picked a worse day, since the date chosen clashed with a royal wedding and the cup final. Jess couldn't help wondering how many Old Grammarians had been invited to the wedding or were actually attending the Cup Final; surely those merely watching the events on TV would be free by 7.30pm? However, in the end forty people, evidently not ardent royalists or football fanatics, had accepted the invitation to attend Jess's talk, which seemed a very reasonable number.

Jess and Izzy spent the next morning at a local animal sanctuary, bedecked with garish bunting, where the staff had thoughtfully installed a large television for those determined not to miss the royal wedding. There was tea and cake and various craft stalls; Izzy, along with many other dogs, was welcome to attend, and behaved herself fairly well, although she did enter into a noisy dispute with a poodle over a dropped biscuit. After lunch Jess and Izzy moved on to an art exhibition in Thorverton village church, which luckily was also dog friendly. Yet more tea and cake was available, it seemed to be a day for hot beverages, bunting and baking.

Making her way back up the Exe valley, Jess arrived early at the school and drew up in the new car-park on the site of the fondly-remembered old building. Nothing whatsoever remained to indicate that this was the place where thousands of pupils had been educated and hundreds of teachers had worked hard to enable their students to achieve success in exams, sports, drama and other activities. Jess looked around and spotted a single memento of the old days – a copper beech tree standing forlornly where the drive used to be. This was the only reminder of her school days half a century previously. Everything else had been obliterated - the netball court, the gardens, the playground and of course the fine old buildings. Jess was especially sorry to see that the former sixth form centre, an old house named Blagdon which had once been the Mayoral residence of the town, had also vanished without trace.

The evening was still warm, and Jess was reluctant to leave Izzy in the car, so she led her into the building, where people were beginning to gather in the hall. A man came forward to make a fuss of Izzy. She was generally a great hit with men, Jess had noticed; there seemed to be something about Staffordshire Bull Terriers which appealed to men of all ages. This kind man offered to hold Izzy's lead when the time came for Jess to speak. The audience took their seats and Jess was welcomed; she was about to start her talk when the door opened and her brother Jeff came in. Evidently his plans for the weekend had changed and he was unexpectedly able to attend the reunion.

Jess began her talk, explaining that the audience would be invited to contribute their own memories at the end. So much had changed in fifty years, not just regarding the fabric of the building, but also many aspects of school life. In the 1960s corporal punishment was still practised, with errant boys frequently receiving the slipper from 'Sam-the-dap' Leaker or even the cane from the Headmaster. Rules as to school dress were rigorously enforced, with prefects able to insist that any girl suspected of wearing her skirt too short must instantly kneel on the floor and have the height of her skirt hem above the knee checked against a six-inch ruler. This regulation was deployed more often against the pretty girls rather than their less attractive classmates, and would no doubt be deemed sexual harassment these days. Jess had never once been asked to kneel and be measured, but she had worn her skirts longer than most of her contemporaries since she rode her bicycle to school and the combination of mini-skirt and stockings simply would not work on a bike. Health and safety rules were as yet unheard of in the 1960s, with chemistry experiments frequently misfiring, so that entire classes had to be evacuated onto the cricket pitch to avoid the possibility of being overcome by noxious fumes, or suffering the after-effects of a test-tube explosion. The two cocker spaniels belonging to the Domestic Science teacher, which had the run of the cookery room, would nowadays of course be seriously contravening hygiene and safety regulations, so that there would no longer be any danger of tripping over a dog while carrying a scalding pan, or of discovering a canine hair in the soup.

Jess then moved on to a brief consideration of changes in society over the past half century. The advent of the contraceptive pill had caused a stir in the 1960s, with much debate as to who exactly should be entitled to receive it – should it be married women only or anyone who asked? Jess recalled young unmarried women borrowing wedding rings from friends in order to convince doctors to prescribe the Pill. The idea of women being in control of their fertility for the first time had caused widespread consternation. Then there had been various important and far-reaching social reforms concerning divorce, the decriminalisation of homosexuality and abortion law. It was possible for the first time to obtain a divorce without the alleged injured party having to consent, so that a marriage could be dissolved after five years' separation without the spouse's agreement. At the time, this had been dubbed a 'Casanova's charter' by certain sections of the press. Jess's own father Jack had been obliged to remain in his marriage in the 1950s because his first wife had refused to divorce him for adultery. He had been unable to marry Jess's mother until after his first wife had died.

However, the change which Jess's parents had most detested and against which they had vociferously protested had been the lowering of the age of majority from 21 to eighteen. There had been much opposition to the idea of 'children' being given the vote and the right to make their own decisions, especially to decide to marry without parental consent. Jess's mother, Dotey, had not been alone in declaring that so far as she was concerned, children should do as they were told until they were 21, and it would always be 21 in her house, no matter what the law said. When Jess decided to get married at twenty Dotey had wrung her hands in despair and declared that she would have had Jess made a ward of court in order to prevent the wedding if only the old law had still applied. How could anyone so young know their own mind in a matter as important as this? (It turned out that she was right, Jess had not chosen wisely. However, Dotey had not lived to see the marriage end, six years later.)

The other significant change which Jess touched upon was the recognition that women and children and some men were suffering domestic abuse. When sixteen year-old Jeff had cycled to the local police station at dead of night, in an attempt to get help to prevent Dotey's husband from beating her, officers declined to attend, stating that they had no powers to intervene in a domestic matter. There were no help-lines or refuges then available in Devon and the first UK Women's Refuge was only just opening in London. Jess had been strictly forbidden by Dotey to speak of any problems at home to outsiders, but in utter despair one day she had confided in Miss Gillen, the history teacher, who had listened carefully. On hearing that Jess was regularly turned out of the house to do her homework in the fields, Miss Gillen had made her attic room available to Jess as a safe place in which to study. Domestic abuse and coercive control were still facts of life in the twenty-first century, but at least they was now recognised as crimes, and there were some resources available for victims. On this note Jess ended her talk and invited contributions from the audience. There were several comments and anecdotes, everyone appeared to have enjoyed Jess's presentation and it had also given them food for thought. At the end, the audience applauded and Jeff came forward to congratulate his sister.

"That went well!" he exclaimed in surprise, much to Jess's amusement. She thought that maybe Jeff had crept in late fearing that she would let the side down in some way, by putting on a poor show, perhaps by mumbling or stumbling over her words, being a boring speaker or forgetting what she meant to say. Jess then rescued Izzy from her helpful handler; the little dog had behaved beautifully during the talk and now joyfully barked her congratulations, since of course Izzy always had complete confidence in Jess.

Tiverton Grammar School -1967

Can you remember, it's so long ago, the years go fast but the days went slow, we sat in the hall in desks in a row to sit our exams at A and O; and the play that year was 'Love on the Dole' starring Andy Lund and Gillian Crowle, I played Mrs. Jike, an old Cockney hag, and the whole of the cast was singing 'The Red Flag'... You haven't forgotten, I'm sure I can't, that a classmate married Cary Grant and went to live in Hollywood- a fairytale of 'local girl makes good'.

Do you remember the chemistry class, heating up stuff in tubes of glass til the fumes and flames made us cough and itch so that everyone ran for the cricket pitch? The cookery room where those spaniels ran about, until Mrs. Lamb made me let them out, to relieve themselves on the hockey pitch? (the dog called Pogo and Polly was the bitch).
Gossip in the library about the latest romances, and Mr. Leaker's Friday country dances, and Mr. Thomas always calling me Frances, though I am dark and she was fair, so I'm not quite sure what was going on there... and rules about skirt lengths, and the length of boys' hair, and the exact shade of green of the jumpers we could wear...

Mr. Wotton, swooping through the door in the academic dress that the teachers still wore; and little 'Ghosty' Armstrong teaching us Latin, looking far too small for the large car he sat in, always parked under the copper beech tree, which still is there for all to see. So much has gone; but at least that tree has lasted throughout half a century, a reminder of what used to be, when we were young in the 'swinging' sixties.

Now we are in our sixties, the time has flown and our old school building has been knocked down. And although the thought causes us all much pain, our memories will still remain.

Chapter 26

Facebook had brought Jess the news of a rally to be held in London marking one hundred years of votes for women. This was a subject of great interest to Jess, who always made a point of voting. She recalled how women had chained themselves to railings, endured imprisonment and brutal forced feeding, while Emily Wilding Davidson had thrown herself under the King's horse with fatal consequences in order to highlight the injustice of the vote being denied to half the population. This had occurred during the lifetime of Jess's mother Dotey, born in 1910; she had therefore attained her majority aged 21 in 1931, being among the first group of women to be universally enfranchised. Jess had tried to locate her mother and her family on the 1911 census records, released to the public after a century, but could find no trace of either Dotey nor grandmother Olivia. Grandfather George was there, with other family members, but not his wife or daughter. Jess concluded that her grandmother must have been in sympathy with the suffragette cause, since one of their protests had centred around the 1911 census, with women declaring that as they were denied the vote then they should not be counted as citizens. It was an offence to be deliberately omitted from the census so women had camped in fields or hidden away in order to be left out of the official count. (Emily Wilding Davidson had managed to hide herself overnight in a cupboard at the House of Commons, where there is now a commemorative plaque, installed after a campaign by Tony Benn.) Jess never met her grandmother, who had died in the 1940s, and thought she would have loved to have had the opportunity to talk with her and to find out why she had not been listed – was it simply an oversight or a deliberate course of action by a suffragist sympathiser?

Another trip to London meant that she would be able to see Tom again so Jess booked her train tickets and set off, leaving Izzy with Nick. Jess had an unusual errand in London; despite the record-breaking heat, she had in her suitcase three mink garments - a coat, a jacket and a stole, the property of Nick's late mother Eunice. It seemed that scarcely anyone wanted furs these days, and not even the local charity shops or theatrical costume agencies would take them, although all were in good condition. Jess had phoned furriers all over the North of England who told her that they dealt only in new items, and were not interested in second-hand items. She had eventually been told of someone in St. John's Wood who would be prepared to look at them with a view to re-sale in Italy, where it seemed that people did not harbour the same aversion to fur as did the British. Jess recalled witnessing the *passagiata* on various Italian trips during the 1990s, where everyone came out in the early evening attired in their finest clothes and paraded along the sea-front or up and down the main street. Furs had always featured prominently, despite the warmth of the weather. It appeared that many Italian women still liked to have a touch of mink slung across their shoulders.

Jess was unfamiliar with St. John's Wood and after alighting from the bus had some difficulty locating the street where the furrier had his shop. After a couple of false starts, she asked two security guards standing outside a synagogue, and they kindly directed her to the correct side street. Jess entered the open door of the shop, but there seemed to be no-one around. She made her way between heavily laden racks of assorted furs through the shop, where the furrier was discovered in a back room, brewing tea. He nodded approvingly when Jess showed him the light-coloured mink jacket. "Ah, Blonde!" He carefully examined the three garments she had brought and gave her a likely selling price, explaining that his commission would be 20%. This seemed to be rather high, but Jess felt that she had no choice; the furs had been stuck in a cupboard for many years and were now at risk of attack from the moth; a recent outbreak of the dastardly creatures had destroyed a woollen jacket of Jess's, and she knew Nick wanted to re-home the furs before any similar disaster might occur. The furrier gave her a receipt and Jess made her way across town with a much lighter suitcase.

Before the suffrage celebration march, which was to be held the following day, Jess had arranged to meet Emmanuel, a young man who was a fan of her book and had taken the trouble to get in touch with her, via the inevitable medium of Facebook. Jess was always pleased and surprised to discover that her work held such appeal for people who did not fall within her target audience of middle-aged women. She was feeling rather tired and hot after her journey and initially wondered if she was actually up for an hour of conversation with a stranger when all she really wanted was to get to Tom's house for a rest. However, it would seem rude to cancel at the last minute. Emmanuel kindly took her for a drink of iced tea at Patisserie Valerie and told her about his early life in Sri Lanka; Jess soon discovered that he was also a dog-lover, so they found that they got on very well despite the differences in age and life-style. Emmanuel explained that after reading and enjoying Jess's book he had written a review on his blog, which had thousands of followers. Jess thanked him, and hoped that his efforts would bring her further sales.

Tom was his usual welcoming self and supplied more cold drinks and a refreshing salad. He was interested to hear of the expedition to the furrier and the chat with the young Sri Lankan, and recalling her previous visit to attend an anti-austerity demonstration, pointed out that most people's mothers up in London for the weekend went shopping or visited museums and galleries or saw a show. With Jess it seemed to be mainly demonstrations, with the odd gruelling cookery lesson and trip to an old-fashioned furrier thrown in...

"You must have been on quite a few marches in your time, Mum; I seem to remember you taking me on one or two when I was young."

"Yes, CND was revived in the 1980s, so we went on a few demos before Alex was born. And of course I attended the Stop The War march in 2003 and that Anti-austerity rally. I suppose there will always be something to demonstrate about – climate change is at the forefront of people's minds at the moment of course, but I've not yet been on any of those marches."

"Excuse for a future visit," said Tom, handing her a cup of tea.

The Suffrage centenary rally was scheduled to start in Park Lane, where the thousands of assembled women were each issued with a scarf in either purple, white or green, the suffragette colours. (White symbolised purity, green for hope and purple for dignity.) Jess was given purple. The idea was for the women to wear the scarves across their shoulders forming three wide strands of colour marching on Westminster. Jess noted that a few women had come attired in Edwardian dress, although the majority, like herself, wore their ordinary clothes. Some carried elaborate banners, embroidered with slogans of the time or representing Trade Unions. There were even a few dogs in with coloured ribbons attached to their collars. Jess was worried that they might struggle in the heat and was relieved to see the owners stopping to give them water. It was yet another scorching day, and marching along Pall Mall was like wading through a canyon of heat. Jess had started out quite near the front, walking with a woman from Australia who was touring Britain However, when the march reached Trafalgar Square, Jess decided that she needed a break, her feet were beginning to swell and her legs ached so that a rest seemed advisable. She rang Tom with a progress report, then bought an expensive ice-cream from the café in the square and sat down to watch the march proceeding down Whitehall. After ten minutes Jess was able to rejoin the end of the procession as it made its way past the gated end of Downing Street and on to the Palace of Westminster. Then everyone went to pay their respects to Emmeline Pankhurst, whose statue was in nearby gardens, before the rally dispersed. It had been such a joyful and good-humoured event, Jess was pleased to have taken part, despite near heat exhaustion.

Back at Tom's house, after a restorative rest and late tea, Jess looked at the pictures of the day's events posted on line; she was amazed to see the overhead shots showing the bands of the three suffragette colours streaming through central London in continuous lines of purple, green and white. A century of women's suffrage had been duly commemorated, and there had been similar rallies in Edinburgh, Cardiff and Belfast. Jess wondered what her grandmother Olivia would have made of it, and concluded that -since she had apparently been prepared to commit an offence by deliberately leaving herself and her daughter out of the 1911 census enumeration - she would in all likelihood have warmly applauded the women's current efforts.

Chapter 27

People sometimes characterised Jess's stories of life in Berringden Brow as being 'too cosy' but these were people who had not read them properly. Village dwellers have all kinds of problems, as do some people everywhere else. Jess had written about the plight of older people whose care services had been discontinued, of domestic violence, homelessness, drug use and alcoholism. Living in a semi-rural location did not serve to protect people from life's hardships.

A current example was a situation in the next street, where Jess's friend Pat was practically living under siege since the arrival of a new tenant in the house opposite. One of the long-term residents, Juliet, had gone to Australia for six months and rented out her house on a short-term tenancy to a young woman with a seven-year-old daughter. The letting agency had asked for references but it turned out that these are nowadays freely available on the internet and the agency had not bothered to check the veracity of those supplied by the young woman, who was known as Squizz. She was keeping a disorderly house, with people arriving at all times of the day and night to obtain drugs. There seemed to be a continual commotion in the street, with people shouting and car tyres screeching. Squizz frequently forgot to collect her daughter from school, so that the Head Teacher had been obliged to bring the child home on several occasions. There was also a shadowy resident male, who at one point was seen dangling the family's pit bull terrier from an upstairs window. Pat had rung the police and community support officers but Squizz seemed to be a law unto herself and blithely ignored all their warnings. Jess had seen her from time to time striding around the village with trailing skirts, long lank hair, dangling earrings and nose piercings. Now it seemed that the child had been taken into care and everyone hoped that she was being properly looked after by a kind foster family. The dog had also disappeared and Jess prayed that this was because the RSPCA had managed to find it a loving home.

Squizz's unruly clients parked without thought for the neighbours and were often rude to anyone who tried to remonstrate with them.

Pat had taken to using her back door so as to avoid them, and had not been into her front garden for several months. Home-owner Juliet had recently returned from Australia and was seeking possession of her house, since the six-month let had run its course, but Squizz was digging her heels in and refusing to vacate the property. Juliet was currently staying with relatives while urgently seeking a court order to evict Squizz and the dog-dangling man.

Jess herself had recently had trouble with a neighbour, who held her responsible for his dog breaking its leg. This temperamental animal, which spent its days guarding the back gate and barking at everyone who passed, had reacted badly when Jess and Izzy came by on their way to the park; the neighbour's dog had then fallen down some steps and injured itself. The neighbour had appeared in Jess's yard and castigated Jess for walking that way up the street, saying she should have used the long way round in order not to upset his animal. Jess of course would not have wished harm on any dog, but did not see how she could be held responsible for the accident. Izzy had not provoked the other dog in any way. The neighbour was thoroughly unpleasant, verging on the downright nasty to Jess, which alarmed her, so that she sought advice from the Dogs Trust, of which she was a member. Their legal officer confirmed that she could not be held to be at fault since she and Izzy had been walking along a public road.

However, despite these unpleasant incidents, there were many good things about living in Berringden Brow, thought Jess one morning, as she hurried off off to help deliver a hot lunch to local housebound and lonely older residents. The quaintly named Old Peoples' Welfare Committee, formed a hundred years previously to provide treats and charabanc outings for old folk, had recently been resurrected, since the plight of lonely people was becoming more evident; indeed some experts were now characterising loneliness as a disease with harmful consequences, both physical and mental. A woman named Lhamo now living in Hebden Bridge but originally from Tibet had kindly offered to cook and pack a hot lunch for seventy older residents identified as being in need, since people living alone often do not feel inspired to cook a proper meal just for themselves. A small army of volunteers was required to transport the lunches before the food became cold and unappetising, and Jess had enrolled.

Jess collected her seven meals – one each for six old people and a spare one for herself, since Lhamo wanted each of the volunteers to also have a meal - and set off with a list of addresses. They were all on a local estate with houses and flats for people aged over sixty, which Jess had never previously visited, although she had frequently walked past with Izzy. To her dismay, Jess found that the numbering of the residences in the complex was very strange. Instead of one side of a street being the odd numbers with the even numbers on the opposite side, it turned out that the entire estate was split in two, with all the odd numbers in one half and all the evens in another, meaning that Jess was obliged to rearrange the proposed delivery route to avoid the necessity of having to yo-yo from one side of the estate to the other. The organisers had provided insulated bags, but even so, Jess was aware that time was going on and people would be looking forward to their hot lunches, not tepid fare.

Jess managed to work out what she imagined would be a more sensible route but was perplexed to find that a street of even numbers ended at 96, when she was looking for 104. She asked a passing lady who was walking a dog if she knew where 104 might be, but the lady replied that although she had lived on the estate for twenty years she had never managed to get to grips with the numbering system, and knew only how to reach her own house. Entering the relevant postcode on her phone did not help either, since the entire estate apparently had the same postcode. Jess was now reduced to knocking on doors and asking surprised residents if they knew how to get to number 104. Eventually she found a kind couple who explained that the house Jess wanted was actually in the street behind theirs; they offered to let her take a short cut through their house, but entering anyone's home was discouraged under the rules of the Old Peoples' Welfare Committee.

Jess ran to the end of the street as quickly as she could, encumbered as she was by the bulky insulated food bag, and recommenced her search for No. 104. However not all of the houses displayed numbers of their doors, in fact very few were clearly indicated, so she again came to a halt. Discovering a house labelled 102, Jess sighed with relief and knocked on the next door. A elderly lady using a walking frame eventually answered her knock, so Jess handed over the meal.

"But I haven't ordered anything!" exclaimed the lady in surprise. Jess explained that someone, a friend or relative perhaps, must have ordered the food on her behalf. The lady took the food parcel and retreated back inside, still shaking her head in wonder. Jess then heard a voice calling to her from a nearby garden.

"Have you got my dinner, lovey?"

"What number are you, please?"

"104. I should be on your list..."
"Oh dear: I thought this house was 104."

"That's 100. I'm 104. Do you have my dinner there, only I'm quite hungry and we diabetics have to eat at regular times, or our blood sugar gets dangerously low..."

Jess realised that she had delivered in error to the house on the right of 102 instead of turning left. No wonder the lady at 100 had seemed surprised. Luckily, Lhamo had provided the spare meal, intended for the volunteer. Jess knew she must surrender her own lunch to the resident of No. 104.

"Sorry it's taken me so long to get here, but lots of the houses in this street don't seem to have a number."

"They're numbered at the back, so you should have come down the back lane."

"Well, I'll know in future!" said Jess. Meals on wheels was turning out to be rather harder than she had imagined. Whoever had taken it

114

upon themselves to number the estate in such an idiosyncratic manner was definitely having a laugh at the expense of delivery people and deserved a piece of her mind, and certainly no hot dinner. Jess had been looking forward to her Tibetan lunch, and would now have to return home and open a tin of soup.

That evening Zofia rang Jess, sounding rather agitated.

"Jess you must bury that orgonite I gave you for Mothering Sunday. The man who made it has been sacked from work, it seems he was thinking evil thoughts and imparting negative energy when he made the orgonites so they won't be any help, in fact they may be harmful. The only way to safely get rid of yours is to bury it deep down as far away as possible from your house. I'm sending Alex over to bury it in the woods, I shan't be happy until I know it's out of your house."

Jess still had the harmless-looking object on her desk, and had not so far noticed any unpleasant or suspicious effects, but when Alex arrived with a spade she handed over the orgonite and let him take it away for disposal in a remote part of the woods, where any damaging emanations would not reach her. Zofia phoned again to check that this had been completed and was relieved to hear that the object was now at a safe depth and distance from Jess and everyone else in Berringden Brow. Jess hoped that any woodland creatures, such as deer, foxes, rabbits, badgers, squirrels or insects which happened to be passing the orgonite burial site would take no harm from its harmful emanations.

Chapter 28

Alex and Zofia had been allocated an allotment. With the increasing popularity of 'grow your own' initiatives, there was such a high demand for plots that they were being divided in half, so that the area was not very large; however, as they surveyed it with Jess, they noted there were an awful lot of weeds to be dealt with including thistles, dandelions and ground elder.

"We're trying the 'no-dig' method, which suffocates the weeds," declared Alex. "We need tons of cardboard to spread over the earth, and I know where there's a skip full of the stuff, outside a take-away in the village. Come on Mum, let's get it before someone else does."

Accordingly, Jess drove Alex to Lower Berringden and parked beside a huge skip, overflowing with squashed cardboard boxes. Alex began loading up the campervan, while Jess remained at the wheel, intending to quickly drive off if someone complained. Two men came out of the takeaway shop, and Jess thought they might be going to rebuke Alex for removing their stuff, but to her relief they began instead to help him load yet more cardboard.

"We have to pay to dispose of it, it's classed as trade waste, so we're only too glad that someone actually wants it!" said one of the men. "We get boxes and boxes of onions and such-like every week, so do spread the word among the allotment friends, if they need any more."

Jess thought how very like Alex this was, not only did he get something for free, but he received help from complete strangers. Jess's friend Hamish always remarked that if Alex fell into the canal he'd come up smiling with a new coat. Alex was the sort of person for whom dropped toast always fell butter side up. Some people seem to lead charmed lives; Jess did not know why Alex was so fortunate, but was simply glad that this was the case.

Back at the allotment, Alex spread the cardboard over the plot, then watered it thoroughly until it became a soggy mulch. He had ordered a load of rotted manure, due to arrive the following week, and hoped to create a fertile growing medium. Jess was interested to see this labour-saving method of weed control, and hoped it would quickly achieve the desired effect so that the crop planting could soon begin. She looked forward to tasting the results of Alex and Zofia's horticultural labours in due course.

At home, Jess was changing the bedding in Nick's attic room when she came across her copy of a book of poems by Pablo Neruda with various bits of paper sticking out from between the pages. Jess had bought the book after seeing the film *Il Postino* about Nobel Laureate Neruda's life in exile on an Italian island, and his friendship with the postman. It was her favourite film. She wondered what had inspired Nick's sudden interest in Neruda, and what was all this paper, covered in his handwriting? Leafing through, she discovered several old envelopes with erotic words in Spanish; Jess could make out "seducir", "servicios sexuales", "sentir atraccion", "no tengo novia" (I don't have a girlfriend) - amongst reminder notes to pay a credit card bill and the council tax. Also on the bedside table was a guide book to Colombia and a Spanish dictionary. Jess went downstairs where Nick was watching racing from Pontefract on TV. Jess knew better than to talk to him mid-race, but after the favourite had won by a short head and the adverts had come on she decided to ask about his sudden interest in Spanish erotic poetry and Colombia.

"Oh..." said Nick. "I've got a Colombian penfriend."

"Indeed? And how did you meet this person?"

"Well, I signed up to an introduction agency, by accident...."

Jess laughed. "How could anyone possibly do such a thing 'By Accident?' And who is this penfriend – she's female, I take it?"

"She's a thirty-year old sports scientist, Paola, from Medellin."

"Thirty! And you're seventy, so she's young enough to be your daughter or even grand-daughter."

"She doesn't mind. Anyway she thinks I'm only sixty...I decided to knock a few years off my real age as I don't look seventy. In any case, the agency match people very carefully."

"And I thought it was only women who lied about their age! What exactly are her interests? Does she like horse-racing?"

"No... she likes cycling, yoga and growing cannabis to make healing potions. And she has a dog. I told her I look after a dog sometimes."

"Well, she'll fit very nicely into this family, won't she – doing yoga with Zofia, cycle rides with Tom, and concocting healing cannabis potions with Alex. I can take her for dog walks with Izzy, then you and she can spend cosy evenings reading Pablo Neruda together."

"She says can't come here at the moment but I'm hoping to go over there, you can fly direct to Colombia from Manchester for only £600 or so. Maybe next year."

"Do you have a picture of her, by any chance?"

Nick brought out his phone and showed Jess a photograph of a beautiful young woman with a long dark hair, a pale oval face and large brown eyes.

"She's very lovely; I suppose it hasn't crossed your mind to wonder what she might see in a septuagenarian who doesn't speak the same language?"

"She doesn't want a Colombian boyfriend because she says they just want women for the kitchen and bedroom. The agency translates our messages."

"Do you have to pay for this service?"

"Yes, but it's not really very much...."

"Haven't you tried to contact her directly, or on social media?"

"That's not how it works, and not everyone does Facebook. I don't!"

"Your profile is on Facebook, even though you don't often post. And what about WhatsApp?"

"But I never use social media!"

Jess sensed that Nick was becoming impatient with her and decided to cease questioning him. After all, he was free to do whatever he wanted with his life and his money. She recalled that he had form when it came to attractive young women – Jess would never forget how Nick abandoned her and young Alex in Zimbabwe, in order to spend a week in the township at Victoria Falls with a woman called Jennifer, to whom he had been introduced by a man at the camp-site bar. He had told Jess he would be out for only an hour and had not thought to notify Jess of his change of plan. In those pre-mobile phone days Jess had no idea of his possible whereabouts, fearing that he might have fallen in the Zambezi or been devoured by a crocodile. She had been at a loss to know where to start searching for him and anyway her responsibility was to look after eleven-year-old Alex. Meanwhile, as it later turned out, Jennifer's many relatives had been busy running up enormous bills at the various night spots in the town leaving Nick to collect the tab. The relatives had also suggested that the pair should get married before Nick was due to leave Victoria Falls to return to Bulawayo, but somehow he had resisted. When the relatives had at last driven Nick back to the camp-site at the end of the week in order to collect his things, Jess was relieved to see him but had understandably given him a piece of her mind, so much so that one aunt had taken Alex aside and asked in shocked tones, who was that woman and why was she so cross with Nick? Was she Nick's wife, as really only a wife could be so annoyed with a man... And was Alex Nick's son? Nick had not mentioned to his new friends that he was travelling with a woman and young child.

Then there had been the time in Bali many years ago when Jess was once more abandoned while Nick and his friend Hesketh went off to the bright lights, only for Hesketh to return drunk, late at night, and without Nick, whom he reported had been last seen 'going off with shome woman.' Nick had reappeared the following morning in a befuddled state, wailing 'she's taken all my money.' Jess calculated that the thousands of Indonesian rupiah Nick had lost amounted to the equivalent of only £17 sterling, so quite a cheap escapade, all things considered. Luckily a quick search of Nick's bag revealed that he had left his British money safely at the hotel. Jess herself had spent a pleasant evening walking on the beach watching the tropical sunset. She really did not understand this urge of Nick's to rush off to find the nearest brothel the minute his feet touched foreign soil, but wondered if it had anything to do with the fact that he had lived at home with his mother until her death when Nick was 57; his mother, Eunice had once told Jess that Nick had never brought any woman home - except Jess herself of course, and she clearly didn't count. Jess had long ago realised that she was being prepared to take over where Nick's mother left off. She wondered what Eunice would have had to say about the Colombian beauty, and the possibility of South American grandchildren. Eunice had been rather set in her ways, but surely any adorable Latin babies would have melted her heart. Jess realised she was running ahead since Nick had not met Paola yet.

"Catfishing!" exclaimed Alex and Zofia in unison. Jess was unfamiliar with the term so Alex explained that it applied to a romantic scam, where the supposed girlfriend does not actually exist. 'Her' messages are composed by the scammer, and often a request for money is sent, or the subscriber is encouraged to buy as many credits as possible to continue the correspondence. It was a well-known phenomenon and had actually happened to a friend of Zofia's whose paramour was also a Colombian beauty. It had not ended well. Jess hoped things would turn out better for Nick but somehow doubted it. Alex declared that if Nick was planning to visit Colombia, then he would be duty-bound to accompany him as his Minder, since the street-wise Alex, although half Nick's age, would be better able to save him from the dangers of an exotic drug and crime filled city.

Chapter 29

At teatime there was a loud knock at the door. Izzy barked frantically, until Jess opened the door to her neighbour, Pam.

"Jess, there's a pit-bull dog next door at Abby's, he rushed into her house and almost knocked over her little boy, but we managed to chase him out and shut him in the yard. Have you any idea who he belongs to? He hasn't got a a collar, just a broken string lead. He's so strong-looking, we're quite afraid of him. Abby's rung the police."

Jess went into the back street and sure enough, there was a light brown pit-bull terrier peering over next door's gate gate and whining. It seemed to be looking for someone. Jess wondered whether the animal was thirsty, so she ran back home and fetched a bowl of water, which she pushed under the gate. The dog at once drank the bowl dry, and Jess was pleased to have been able to alleviate its immediate distress. She went to fetch more water and wondered if she should try to take the dog to a vet who could scan its microchip ID, which all dogs are required to have by law. However, she felt nervous about approaching such a strong and distressed animal.

Jess decided that she would put a notice on the village Facebook page, appealing for its owner to come forward, since this method of reuniting animals and owners often worked well for stray dogs and cats. A woman replied at once saying that she was very experienced with animals and was willing to collect the dog and take it to the vets for scanning, so Jess went to tell Abby and Pam. She knocked on Abby's front door, but there was no reply, so she went round the end of the terrace and into the back street. There she found the two women and a community support officer, with the dog, who was being comforted by a man bending over it, presumably the owner. As Jess approached, the man looked up and her first impression was of deep-set blue eyes in a gaunt face. Jess had not seen him before.

The man was explaining that he had recently moved into a nearby street, from which Jess gathered that he was in Russ's old house. The dog had broken its leash and escaped from the yard where he had been fastened. Being unfamiliar with the area, he did not know his way back home.

Jess said that she had given the dog water and that a local woman had offered to take it for scanning. The gaunt man shook his head.

"Would have been no use, he's not chipped. I can't afford it."

"Well, I'm sure some charities do pet micro-chipping quite cheaply, you ought to get it done to comply with the law and in case he escapes again. Then he can soon be brought back without any fuss."

Jess was aware she was sounding rather like an old-fashioned schoolmistress scolding a naughty pupil. While the community support officer was making notes, Jess hastily reached for her phone and posted on Facebook that the dog's owner had been traced. She watched the man lead the dog away by his broken string lead which was clearly not going to be of much future use. Jess remembered that she had a strong collar and stout lead in her shed, these items had belonged to her previous beloved dog, Mash, and were not needed for Izzy, who had her own harness and lead. Jess picked up the water bowl and returned home. A few minutes searching in the shed revealed what she was looking for, although the leather collar needed cleaning. Jess wiped it thoroughly and went round to Russ's house, which of course was now the home of the gaunt man and his pit-bull terrier. Jess hoped that the sudden departure of Russ did not mean that he was again incarcerated in Hull jail. She knocked on the door and heard the dog bark, but there was no other response. She knocked again, and the man's head appeared at an upstairs window. He peered cautiously at Jess, who held out the collar and lead.

"I've brought you these, in case they're of any use. They belonged to my previous dog and I don't need them," Jess called up to him.

The man nodded and said he would come down. The door opened and he came out, closing the door behind him, explaining that he could not ask Jess in since the dog did not care much for strangers. Jess handed him the collar and lead and the man thanked her.

"We've a supportive dog-walking community round here, we meet up on the field across the road, you're very welcome to join us..."

The man shook his head. "Mine can't go out anywhere grassy, he had parvo virus last year and very nearly died. The vet said he's not allowed to go out until the autumn in case he picks something up."

"Oh, poor thing! No wonder he was keen to escape from your yard. He must hate being cooped up. What's his name? How old is he?"

"He's called Dino and he's three; he's not even my dog, but my friend couldn't cope with him so I said I'd take him. Since then there's been nothing but illness and trouble. He comes to work with me and swims in the river next to my workshop sometimes. He enjoys that."

Jess was pleased to hear that Dino had some enjoyment in his life. However, the man had just said he worked, yet he had told her that he could not afford a pet microchip, which seemed rather odd. Jess had assumed he must be unemployed. Surely a working man would be able to afford a decent collar and lead for his dog? Unless he was self-employed and barely making a living. Jess knew from her advice work days that it was often hard for people in such a situation. She turned to leave, but the man seemed keen to continue their chat.

"I've not long been back in the UK, I was working in South Africa."

Jess was interested to hear this. "I was in South Africa briefly, on a holiday to Cape Town during the time I was staying in Botswana, more than twenty years ago now. What work did you do out there?"

"I was with an organisation which rescues animals. Do you remember hearing about a large oil-spill off Cape Town? I helped save the penguins, there were thousands of them to be cleaned up."

Jess recalled seeing the African penguins on Boulder Beach, She would have liked to chat for longer and learn more about the life of the gaunt man, but she remembered Izzy at home, wanting her tea, and also Dino indoors, probably also waiting to be fed. She turned towards the gate once more, but the man continued.

"I married an African woman out there, but she didn't like the idea of living here, it's too cold for her, so now we're getting divorced."

"I'm sorry to hear that," murmured Jess.

"So now I'm depressed," went on the man. Jess noted the sadness in his eyes. She realised that he must be finding it difficult to cope, and regretted the way she had told him off about the lack of a microchip.

"Well, if you think I can help in any way, do let me know. It's a friendly neighbourhood and I hope you soon settle in."

The man shrugged. "I haven't found it very friendly so far. I had the police round the other day searching the house for cannabis. Seems that someone had reported me for having a grow in the attic…"

"Goodness, did they find anything?" asked Jess.

"Of course not, I don't even use the stuff, let alone grow it!"

"Well, lots of people round here do, you can smell it as soon as you step outside, so I suppose someone's given the the wrong house number. I was reported for playing loud music, but in fact the culprit was my neighbour. Some people take it upon themselves to act as local guardians but don't always check their facts. I know it can be annoying. By the way, I'm Jess, I live at No.10 on the front street."

"And I'm Ryan," said the man with a slight smile.

"Well Ryan, I hope you and Dino will be happy here, despite a rather rocky start."

Jess returned home and looked up the numbers of local animal welfare organisations offering cheap micro chipping. She wrote down the information; it was up to Ryan whether he wanted to act upon it, but Jess reflected that since he had worked with animal welfare groups in Africa he must surely have Dino's best interests at heart. Jess also found the number of a local support group aimed at helping people living with depression, so added this to the list. She ran round and pushed the paper through Ryan's letterbox.

The Film Club offering this month was *An Education* about a bright 1960s schoolgirl seduced by a charming conman. Coincidentally, the main character, Jenny, has a controlling father named Jack, as indeed had Jess; but that was where the similarities ended, since Jenny was beautiful and Jess's teenage awkwardness had continually been remarked upon by her parents. Jess knew that, had a conman tried to obtain the trust of her parents, they would not have been taken in as had Jenny's mother and father. Her own father's first reaction would have been to question how any man could possibly want to take an interest in the lumpen Jess, while her mother Dotey, who had had bad experiences in her own love life, had come to suspect all men of duplicity and had therefore decreed that Jess would never marry, being too plain and ungainly. Jess was destined to become a headmistress or an academic blue-stocking, declared Dotey, very pleased to have thus disposed of her daughter's future. She had not lived to see Jess's many scrapes and misadventures, which was maybe just as well. Jess knew that before she got to heaven, even if St. Peter was quite happy for her to enter the pearly gates, Dotey would be ahead of him with a stern expression and a long list of the things she, Jess, had not done correctly in life according to her mother's exacting standards, so that Jess would be obliged spend eternity listening to Dotey's litany of complaints. Jess was therefore determined to live as long as possible in order to delay the awful hour of maternal judgment.

Chapter 30

By early autumn, Jess began to wonder about the blackberries in Ryan's garden. The previous occupant, Russ had let her pick them, and as Jess walked past with Izzy she noted that Ryan did not seem to want them and all the ripe fruit was dropping onto the ground. Jess hated to see good berries going to waste, so she knocked on Ryan's door. To her surprise, there was no sound of Dino barking and Jess wondered what had become of him. It would surely soon be time for him to be released from quarantine. Jess knew Ryan was at home because his van was parked outside the house. Perhaps he was in the attic and had not heard her knock. She tried again and Ryan eventually appeared, still looking sad and gaunt.

"Hello Ryan, I hope you don't mind me asking, but if you don't need all these blackberries, I wonder if I could pick some of them? I usually make bramble jelly for friends and family and it seems a shame to waste them."

Ryan nodded. "Come and get them any time. Oh, I never thanked you for your note. I suppose should have come round."

"That's quite OK. And how's Dino? Did you get him chipped?"

"Actually, the RSPCA came and took him away. I wasn't feeling well enough to cope with him so I surrendered him voluntarily. He needed to be properly rehabilitated and re-homed with someone who was up to it."
"I'm sure they'll find him a good home, he's a nice-looking dog."

Jess did not feel that she could ask whether Ryan had contacted the support group for which she had provided the number, but to her surprise, Ryan himself raised the subject.

"I got in touch with that organisation you told me about, and I'm hoping to start attending their meetings in soon."

"Good, I'm very pleased to hear it. I hope you find them helpful"

Jess turned to go, saying that she would pick the blackberries later that day. Ryan nodded and went back indoor. Jess reflected that he must be rather lonely, on his own in the house without even Dino for company. Izzy was of course all the company Jess needed.

Jess checked to see that Ryan's van was not outside the house before she returned to pick the blackberries. She did not want him to think she was an interfering busybody, or worse still, some kind of stalker. The fruit was especially good this year and soon Jess had filled a container with luscious berries. She was debating whether or not to start on a second container when to her dismay, the van pulled up.

"There's still a lot left," observed Ryan. "I suppose some of them are a bit high up for you to reach. I'll get some steps."

Jess was about to protest that she had sufficient fruit to be going on with but Ryan opened up the van and produced a stepladder. Placing it near the wall, he climbed up and handed the fruit down to Jess.

"This reminds me a bit of picking the marula fruit in South Africa," said Ryan. He descended the step-ladder with the last of the berries.

"I should never have come back. I could have stayed, as I have dual citizenship because of my marriage. My asthma has got a lot worse since I returned."

"Yes, Cape Town has a wonderful climate," agreed Jess. "Although I'm hardly an expert, as I as only there for a short holiday. I think my favourite memory of the city is attending a cathedral service in memory of those who had died of AIDS. Archbishop Desmond Tutu gave the blessing, he said that previously, apartheid had seemed an insurmountable barrier to progress in the country, but that it was at the time being officially dismantled; and then AIDS had become a terrible feature of life in South Africa, but that the disease would also eventually be swept away, God willing…"

"What else did you do during your stay?" asked Ryan.

"We visited Table Mountain and the Kirstenboch Gardens - so very beautiful. One morning we took the ferry to Robben Island and had a conducted tour of the prison by one of the former political prisoners who had been held there, his name was Patrick and I was surprised he had wanted to return to the place where he had been incarcerated but he was keen for everyone to know exactly what it had been like."

"I got married on Robben Island in the year 2000," said Ryan. "Every Valentine's Day they hold a wedding service in the chapel. That year was actually the first time and Nelson Mandela was there with Thabo Mbeke. I was the first white man to be married there."

"Nelson Mandela was at your wedding?" exclaimed Jess. "That's amazing! Do you have any photos I could see?"

Ryan's face clouded. "Well, they're on my computer and I can't get to them at the moment. But if you look on the internet for Robben Island weddings it should come up."

Jess felt that she had been rather tactless, there could be any number of reasons why Ryan did not wish to show her the wedding photographs. He was obviously still upset about the failure of his marriage and maybe felt that Jess was being nosey - Jess herself felt that she had indeed been rather too inquisitive. Or maybe his internet service was down so that the computer was not working. She picked up her blackberry boxes and thanked Ryan for his assistance with picking the fruit, then returned home. That evening she made several jars of bramble jelly, and the following day, having checked that the van was not outside the house, she placed one on Ryan's doorstep.

Chapter 31

It was announced that Richard Hawley was to give a concert in Berringden's magnificent Cloth Hall, an imposing eighteenth century edifice in the Italianate style, with a newly-refurbished courtyard. Jess tried to obtain a ticket but discovered that they had quickly sold out. Then a man in Hebden Bridge posted on Facebook that he had spare tickets since his wife had given birth unexpectedly early and so the new parents would not now be able to attend the concert. He was offering their tickets at a discount price in order that someone else might benefit from them. Jess arranged to collect a ticket and scanned the interminably long list of instructions for those entering the Cloth Hall. There would be a mandatory bag search for everyone; one small water bottle was permitted but no flasks or picnic hampers, no smoking/vaping, flags, alcohol, laser pointers, sharp objects, chairs, bicycles, balls, frisbees, animals, banners, flares, fireworks, aerosols, lanterns, drugs, unauthorised literature (whatever that meant - Jess wondered whether a copy of certain red-top newspapers would be frowned upon and only readers of quality dailies admitted) drones, grenades, air-horns.. On and on went the list, with the litany of prohibited items becoming increasingly improbable, so that Jess decided that none of it could possibly apply to her.

Jess parked at Berringden railway station, and reached for her jacket, since the it was an outdoor event and the evening was chilly. She found to her dismay that she had forgotten to bring it. The only warm item available was Izzy's rather disreputable tartan dog blanket on the back seat, so Jess folded it in half and wrapped round her like a shawl. It had a few holes and looked rather odd but would certainly be better than shivering all evening. Joining the queue of anorak-clad middle-aged Richard Hawley fans outside the Cloth Hall, in good time to get one of the limited seats available, Jess was confronted by an elderly woman in an orange high-viz jacket, who instructed her to turn out her bag. Jess did not imagine she had any contraband, but the woman seized her small collapsible umbrella, declaring that this was on the list of prohibited items and must therefore be confiscated.

"Why are umbrellas not permitted/" asked Jess in astonishment. She had stopped reading the catalogue of banned items before reaching Parasols and Umbrellas. Surely they should have appeared before some of the more unlikely items on the list.

"Could be classed as an offensive weapon!" said the official. Then seeing Jess's look of mixed incredulity and dismay, she whispered, "Just shove it back in the bottom of your bag, love!"

Moving down the line, a further official instructed Jess to remove the top of her plastic water bottle, since it could be used as a missile. As usual at such events, it took quite a while for the sound checks to be completed. Jess chatted to a couple sitting next to her, who had travelled from Llandudno; this was the sixth Richard Hawley concert they had attended. Another woman chimed in that she was from Stafford, and she followed Richard all over the country. Someone else came from Hull. Jess admitted that she lived just a few miles away; she was interested to hear what everyone was saying, and inadvertently placed her half-full open water bottle on the seat. The contents spilled so that the lady from Llandudno had a damp bottom.

"Oh, I'm so sorry," said Jess, trying to mop up with Izzy's blanket. The lady was very gracious, but Jess still felt terrible, and explained that she had been ordered to relinquish the bottle top as a condition of entry. This seemed odd, since the stalls selling drinks inside the Cloth Hall served the bottles complete with lids, despite the fact that they were potential missiles according to the security staff.... Jess then related how on a flight from Canada the steward had spilled scalding hot tea over her lap, so that she had been obliged to wriggle out of her trousers and sit in her knickers under a blanket, her spare clothes being in her suitcase in the hold. The steward had blithely remarked that it was only the second time this had happened during his career, while Jess had spent the remainder of the uncomfortable flight drying out.

With still no sign of the supporting act appearing on stage, and by now feeling rather chilly, Jess decided to buy a cup of hot chocolate. Sure enough, this came with a plastic top, which Jess supposed she could have used as a missile if she chose.

"Now let's see how much damage I can do with this!" said Jess, resuming her seat. A few people nearby giggled but unsurprisingly, her immediate neighbours moved some distance away.

Finally, the stage was set, and after the supporting act (whom Jess thought had a good voice but not much taste in songs) Richard Hawley made an appearance - well worth the wait. The rain had held off, which was a blessing, since, had started, Jess would have been the only audience member with an umbrella, and she would have been too scared to put it up, thereby risking the charge of brandishing an offensive weapon, with who knows what dire consequences.

Chapter 32

Jess and Zofia were traveling to the Wirral to visit Jess's old friend Stella. Stella had fought a long battle with alcohol, but had eventually managed to give up drinking and was now attending a wonderful support project for recovering addicts. This group went on trips to North Wales, took part in Outward Bound sessions, theatre visits, walks, and also ran creative writing groups and many more activities. Stella had benefitted enormously from her attendance and spoke enthusiastically of her adventures with the group. Jess had previously been invited to one of the creative writing group's sessions, since Stella was keen to show the members that she had a published author as a friend. The dozen or so members of the group had all contributed to the session by reading a short piece of their work, some humorous, some thoughtful, and all very moving. However, recently Stella had been having problems with an arthritic knee, severely limiting her mobility and causing her to stay home most of the time, so she was becoming increasingly isolated. She had the use of a three-wheeled walking frame, but complained that she could not get it onto buses, so was unable to reach the centre where the support group met. When Jess phoned her to say that she and Zofia would like to visit, Stella had at first sounded rather unwell and inclined to put them off, but she had later rung back sounding much more cheerful, and asked what time they were coming. Zofia had booked an Airbnb cottage just over the Welsh border so that she and Jess would not have to rush back home. There was no question of them being able to stay with Stella in her one-bedroomed flat.

Stella was pleased to see them and welcomed them into the living room. Jess noted that it was clean and tidy, unlike a previous occasion when Stella had been quite unable to cope with everyday tasks such as cleaning. After that visit, Jess had contacted Social Services, who had promptly responded by sending in care workers once a day to check on Stella, do the shopping and cleaning and generally tidy up. Stella and Jess reminisced about the holidays they had enjoyed together in Italy, and looked at some old photographs of those happy times, while Zofia helpfully hung up some washing and made a cup of tea. Jess was careful not to linger over the photographs which included Jake, Stella's former partner, who had abandoned her during her alcoholic phase, in what Jess considered to have been an extremely callous manner, turning up at Stella's hospital bed and announcing that he refused to have her back in his flat, so that the social workers had been obliged to find her a new place stay once she was discharged. However, on reflection, Jess remembered that alcoholics could often be very difficult to live with, she was aware of this from her own experiences with her father in the 1960s; so perhaps Jake had been at his wits end and completely unable to cope.

Stella turned back to a particularly good picture of herself and Jake which Jess had hurried over and stared at it for a few moments.

"I wonder what Jake's doing nowadays. He'll have retired by now." Jake was seven years younger than Stella, who was now in her mid-seventies, so it seemed reasonable to assume that Jake would now be drawing his pension. Stella seemed reluctant to let go of the picture and asked Zofia to put it on the bookcase opposite her chair where she could look at it at any time.

Jess was keen to distract her friend from thoughts of her lost love, and offered to take Stella down to the sea front, where she could park the car on the promenade and let down the windows so that Stella could enjoy some fresh air, even if she could not manage to get out of the car; Stella thanked her, but said she really did not feel quite up to it. She was looking rather pale and evidently her knee was still very painful. The visitors were mindful that they should not tire Stella, so after they had drunk their tea Jess suggested that they should consider making their way to the Welsh B and B, for a five o'clock check-in.

"She's much better now than when we last saw her, in that dreary respite place," said Zofia.

"Yes, she seems much happier," agreed Jess, recalling with a shudder the alcohol-induced paranoia and bitter outbursts to which Stella had been prone during her drinking days, when she was convinced that her neighbours were spying on her through the electric sockets; she had rung the police on more than one occasion to complain about them, and had phoned Jess at six o'clock one morning, although Jess had been unable to reassure Stella that her neighbours were not spies.

They headed across the Welsh border and up into the Clywiddian Hills, where their B and B was located at the end of a steep remote track next to the Offa's Dyke footpath. They found the place unlocked, so went in, to be immediately greeted by an African Grey parrot in a large cage in the entrance lobby, much to Jess's surprise.

"Hello, how are you?" asked the parrot.

"Oh, yes, I forgot to tell you, the landlady mentioned something about a parrot," said Zofia, bringing their bags in from the car, while Jess filled the kettle. "It's apparently quite vocal and likes to chat to guests, but the woman said we can put a cloth over it to shut it up if we get fed up with its noise."

"What's its name, I wonder?" asked Jess.

"She said it's called Fred. Look, here's the guest book; and everyone seems to have mentioned how much they enjoyed Fred's company."

After a cup of tea, Jess began to cook the evening meal while Zofia switched on the television to watch the news. However, the incessant chattering of the parrot proved rather annoying and they agreed that it was time for Fred to settle down for the night. Fortunately, the cloth placed over the cage worked like magic, so that Fred ceased his squawking and became silent. The pasta was quickly cooked, a jar of sauce opened, a salad assembled; then after the meal Jess was ready to retire to bed with her book and her memories of Stella in Italy, regretting the fact that nowadays Stella did not even feel able to go as far as the bottom of the road to look at the sea. She hoped that next time Stella might be feeling up to a drive and some sea air...
The next morning Jess and Zofia were awakened promptly at eight

o'clock by Fred squawking in his still covered cage, rather like an avian alarm clock. They got up rather reluctantly and had a breakfast of boiled eggs and toast. There were no instructions for feeding Fred, and Jess supposed the landlady would see to him after they had left.

"We'd better put something in the guest book," said Zofia.

Jess pondered as to what might be an appropriate entry; she was tempted to write that she would really have preferred the company of a Norwegian Blue, referencing the old Monty Python Dead Parrot sketch, but decided that this would not be very tactful, so instead added a comment about the comfort of the bed and loveliness of the view, disdaining to mention Fred. She supposed that the previous guests who had enjoyed his company must have been parrot fanciers.

The women set off for Holywell, to visit the shrine regarded as the Welsh equivalent of Lourdes. The buildings surrounding the well were impressive, and there were people bathing in the adjacent open-air pool, although the weather was quite chilly. Jess supposed they were taking a cure, or maybe simply enjoying the invigorating sensation of coldwater outdoor swimming, which had recently been suggested as a means of slowing down the progress of dementia.

"We should have brought our swimming costumes," said Zofia.

Jess was quite relieved that they had not, since the pool did not look very inviting. There was a lovely open-air swimming spot with sandy beach and glorious views on the moors above the Berringden Valley, which attracted crowds despite its remoteness. Families gathered for swimming, paddling, splashing and picnics, everyone unfazed by the presence of the naked old man who habitually disported himself on the shore. Jess had always imagined that nudist beaches were more likely to be found along the South coast, in Brighton or Budleigh Salterton, but reflected that Yorkshire folk were a hardy bunch, and so the opportunity for nude swimming in the chilly, hilly Pennines could be considered as one of the few advantages of global warming.

Chapter 33

Nick's phone was on charge on the kitchen counter while he was out with Izzy. Jess was making scones. The phone pinged and Jess glanced down at it. A text flashed across the screen: "Latin Sensations! Esmerelda wants to send you a message!"

Jess resisted the temptation to see what Esmeralda's message to Nick might be. She realised that Latin Sensations must be the name of the agency that had introduced Nick to Paola, but now it appeared that they were offering to put him in touch with yet another Latin lady. Jess finished her mixing, cut six scones out of the dough and put her baking into the oven. She washed her hands and made a cup of tea before checking the internet. The feed-back from subscribers to the Latin Sensations agency was not encouraging, with the site attracting only a single star rating out of a possible five. One man said he had wanted to give the agency zero stars but this was apparently not an option. Several irate and disappointed men had written that Latin Sensations was a hoax, with paid employees writing the messages to gullible subscribers, and false pictures being issued of beauties who could easily have been models rather than women actually seeking British partners. All the women seemed to have interesting and important jobs such as doctors, scientists, vets, TV presenters, engineers and diplomats. There did not appear to be any ordinary-looking women or down-to earth occupations represented and the men reviewing the site stated that it all sounded too good to be true, because it was a scam, intended to get people to buy credits in order to continue a fictitious romance by text. Any request to have direct contact by email or WhatsApp was refused, an excuse was made as to why this was not possible at the present time. Several men had actually flown out to Colombia to meet their girlfriends, but none had succeeded, the habitual excuse for the no-shows being that a relative had been shot.

Jess's heart sank with dismay, since she knew that Nick was planning to fly out to Colombia the following year. What would happen to him in Medellin if Paola was not real? He would be heart-broken and alone in a strange and possibly dangerous city. Maybe he should consider taking up Alex's offer to accompany him as his Minder? Jess hoped that Nick might agree to this, since the thought of a vulnerable septuagenarian on the autistic spectrum wandering alone friendless in the former drug capital of South America horrified her. Another ping sounded, but this was the oven timer, indicating that the scones were ready. Jess retrieved them from the oven, perfectly risen and browned, and put them on a wire rack to cool. She was just making herself a cup of tea when Nick and Izzy returned from their walk, no doubt lured home by the smell of baking, so it was hot buttered scones all round, and Jess could not bring herself to mention her investigations into Latin Sensations; after all, there was no reason why Nick could not himself Google the organisation, should he feel inclined to carry out his own research.

A skip had appeared outside Ryan's house, and a quantity of furniture was being carelessly tossed into it. Jess wondered what had become of Ryan, who had only been living there a short time. Ryan's neighbour Bobby and his dog Stanley came up the street, and Bobby stopped to chat.

"Ryan's had to move out, he wasn't doing well on his own, especially after the dog was taken off him. Poor lad, he's had a lot to cope with, what with leaving South Africa and the break-down of his marriage."

Their conversation was halted by the appearance of two workmen, flinging a large sofa onto the skip. It was upsetting, seeing someone's household effects being disposed of in such a callous manner, and Jess felt quite sad as she continued her walk; despite the fact that she had not known Ryan well she felt concerned about him and hoped that he would be happier in his new life, wherever that may be.

The telephone rang, and Jess answered cautiously, since the man's voice was unfamiliar, and she seemed to receive so many unsolicited calls these days, from people telling her that there was something wrong with her computer, or that her bank account was being compromised. They were all scammers, who appeared to disregard the fact that Jess had registered her number with the telephone preference service. However this man sounded relieved to have made contact with Jess, and introduced himself as Stella's brother, Brian.

"Sad news, I'm afraid; Stella died last Sunday in hospital."

Jess was very shocked, since she had not known that Stella had been taken ill; it was only a few weeks since she and Zofia had visited Stella, who had seemed fairly well at the time apart from her painful knee. Brian was now explaining what had happened. It seemed that Stella had had a fall at home, and been taken into hospital where she had then developed pneumonia and died.

"She's not been well since all that trouble with Jake and then the drink problem. And she was overweight because she couldn't take any exercise with the bad knee...I knew you had visited recently, she told me on the phone, I used to ring once in a while but as you know, we were not close, she was very unpleasant about my wife. So I thought I really should let you know, but it was quite a job because Stella didn't have an address book, everything was in a muddle and I eventually came across your phone number in one of her old diaries."

Jess murmured how sorry she was to hear this sad news and would Brian please let her know when and where the funeral was to be held.

"It's 2pm next Monday at the crematorium. We've booked the small chapel, as we don't imagine there will be many people there. She lost touch with many of her friends during her drinking episode, and we have very few relatives, just a couple of cousins. I don't have Jake's contact details, the number I rang no longer works, so I can't let him know, although he may not in any case wish to attend. What about that support group she used to go to, have you any idea of their number? There might be a few people there who remember Stella."

Jess offered to get in touch with the support group, since she had the contact details of Ned the coordinator, from the time when Stella had invited her to attend one of the the creative writing group's meetings.

Ned was saddened, but not entirely surprised to hear that Stella had died. He had visited her at home a few times after she had stopped attending the group, and thought she sounded quite depressed. He believed that she appeared almost to have given up on many of the things which enhance life, such as friends and interests; and when Jess mentioned that Stella had not wanted to go in the car down to the seafront, he commented that this did not really surprise him.

Brian phoned Jess again to ask if she would care to contribute some memories of Stella for the vicar's address, since Stella had not been a church goer and the vicar had not known her. Jess was happy to recount episodes from their holiday adventures, and also mentioned that Stella had stayed in her house to look after thirteen-year-old Alex while Jess was away in Singapore. Alex and Stella had always got on famously and Alex regarded her as a favourite honorary aunt. Alex, Zofia and Nick would also be attending Stella's funeral.

Jess then turned her attention to the question of Jake. There appeared to be a large number of men with his name on Facebook, far too many profiles for Jess to plough through. Then she remembered that Jake had a daughter, with a very unusual Christian name. Jess typed in the name, and it brought up a single profile. This was indeed Jake's daughter, so Jess sent her a message. Almost immediately, she received a reply, informing her that Jake had died suddenly a few months previously; he had not lived long to enjoy his retirement. Jake's daughter did not go into detail, but merely expressed her condolences that Stella had also now died. Stella had not used any social media and could not have known that when Zofia had placed Jake's photo on the bookcase at her request, he was no longer alive.

Depending on traffic conditions on the motorway, it could be a two hour drive to the Wirrall, so Jess insisted that they set off in plenty of time. Alex said he wanted to go down to the sea, but Jess preferred to leave this until after the funeral. As feared, there were very few people present, since Stella had lost touch with so many friends. Problems with alcohol, loss of mobility and depression had led her to isolate herself, so that the number of mourners was reduced to a mere ten: Brian, his wife and son, plus a cousin and her husband, Jess's family and Ned from the support group.

A forlorn-looking wreath of white lilies was the only floral tribute; (family flowers only had been requested, with cash donations to Age Concern for those who wished to give.) Stella would have preferred something with vivid colours, thought Jess. The well-meaning vicar did her best, but since she had never met Stella her address lacked the personal touch. She mentioned Stella's time as an au pair in Paris, her fluency in French, and the snippet about Stella enjoying looking after Alex when Jess had been away; also her fondness for foreign travel with the northern socialist group, which was where she had met Jess. Jess was then rather startled to hear the vicar talk about about Stella's struggles with alcohol - was this usual in a eulogy, she wondered? She supposed that Brian had wanted the tribute to be an honest account of Stella's life and sadly it was the case that of recent years, drink had played a significant part, undermining her health and possibly hastening her death. She claimed to have given up alcohol, but Brian told Jess that he had found empty bottles in her bedroom.

After the short service Brian thanked everyone for coming. There was no funeral tea arranged, so after a few words with Ned, Jess and her family hurried away. They had left Izzy in the car parked outside the chapel; it was a dull day and the service was scheduled to last only half an hour so there was no danger of Izzy overheating. Jess drove to a country park overlooking the Dee estuary where they could have a quick cup of tea from the flasks she had brought, and then take Izzy down to the beach. They all made their way down a flight of wooden steps to the sand, Alex and Izzy joyfully running ahead. Eventually they reached a rocky promontory barring their way, so were obliged to turn around and head back towards the car park. Alex noticed a blackthorn bush, its branches heavy with dark sloes, and decided to pick them for sloe gin; he had no suitable container so Jess offered him her woolly hat, and they all joined in with the fruit gathering.

The rush-hour traffic was by now building up along the motorway, so it was a further two hours before they reached home. Jess was too tired to cook anything, but fortunately there were some left-overs from the Sunday joint, so with those and bubble-and squeak, followed by a hastily-concocted fruit salad, they made their own funeral tea. Afterwards, Jess retrieved her old photograph albums from the landing cupboard, and they spent an hour looking at the pictures of a once happy Stella, and smiled at their memories.

Chapter 34

Walking Izzy through the woods one teatime Jess recognised Ryan approaching, leading a fine-looking dog. Ryan smiled and stopped to stroke Izzy. He looked much healthier than when Jess had last seen him; his face had filled out a little and had a much better colour.

"Is this a new dog? He's a handsome animal I must say."

Ryan said the dog belonged to a friend, and he was looking after it for the day. The dog had sired pups and it was hoped that one of them would be shown at Crufts the following year.

"How are you, Ryan? I hope things are better for you now."

"Yes, I'm feeling OK now, moved in with a friend, but still attending that support group you told me about. They've helped me a lot."

"Well, that's really good to know. I'm very pleased for you."

Ryan and the dog continued on their walk while Jess and Izzy made for home. Jess felt pleased that she had been able to help Ryan in a small way; however, her contented mood changed as she passed the bus shelter at the end of the road, only to recognise a weeping, shivering figure huddled in the corner under a tatty-looking blanket.

"Ellie, is that you? Whatever's wrong? Where's Dan?"

"He's cashed our Giro and gone off to see a man in Todmorden," sniffed Ellie. "He's left me here with no money and no food."

"But don't you have a house now? Can't you go home?"

"The house got taken off us cos Dan didn't pay the rent. The Giro money was supposed to include rent for us to give to the landlord, but Dan spent it on drugs. And we haven't even got the tent now, he sold it, so we're sleeping rough again..."

Jess noted that Ellie did not appear to have anything with her, no spare clothes nor any bedding apart from the threadbare blanket. She guessed that Dan had sold the couple's belongings.

"Is there anything I can do to help?" asked Jess with a sinking heart, for she had a good idea as to what the answer might be.

"Yea, can you let me have some money, please? That Damien what lives up the road from you spoke to me earlier and he's gone home to fetch me a sleeping bag, so it's just food money I need now. I don't know what time Dan's coming back. He just told me to wait here until he got back, but he's been gone hours and it's getting dark now."

"Oh dear, I'm afraid I don't carry any money with me when I'm walking the dog. I'll have to go home and see what I can find."

Just then Damian arrived, with a warm-looking sleeping bag draped over his arm. Jess imagined that as soon as Dan saw it, he would very likely sell it, so that if Ellie managed to hold onto it for one night that would be something. Damien also handed Ellie a twenty pound note and she smiled with relief.

"Thanks, Damien, that's really great, now I can get some food from the takeaway, I've not had anything to eat today."

Ellie stood up and dusted herself off. She appeared to Jess to be skinnier than ever, her clothes were dirty, her long hair a dull and tangled mass. Jess knew that Social Services would be unlikely to assist now, since Ellie had recently turned eighteen. She was legally an adult, but seemingly still in thrall to Dan. Jess heart ached for the young woman, but there was nothing much that anyone could do to help her while she was still with Dan. He obviously found it useful to have Ellie with him since he could claim extra money as a couple rather than as a single man. The Giro money which was meant to provide for their basic needs - food, shelter and clothing - was wasted on drugs. Jess knew there were Drop-In centres and kind folk such as Damien who were prepared to assist homeless people, and she had heard of a local organisation called Angels which handed out hot drinks and hygiene supplies to rough sleepers, so short-term help was available; but no-one could provide any long-term solutions unless people requested it. Ellie would have to be prepared to finally break with Dan if she was ever to improve her life, yet she appeared to be still totally under his control. Ellie's phone now pinged.

"It's Dan, he says he's on the next bus. I'll tell him to get off at the takeaway and we can have our tea. Thanks again, Damien!"

Ellie walked quickly in the direction of the village centre, hugging the bulky sleeping bag close to her. She had left the scruffy blanket in the bus shelter. Jess wondered whether she should take it home and wash it but decided against any further involvement with the couple. Various statutory and voluntary organisations had tried over the past year to help Ellie without success, and she and Dan were well-known to the Police and Social Services. They both had family living locally but simply did not seem to be ready to accept any help to adopt a more conventional life-style, because Dan liked drugs more than he liked Ellie, or having a place to live, or regular meals.

Hamish phoned to say that he was about to move into sheltered accommodation. Living alone was becoming a struggle, and he felt he now required the support offered by the sheltered flats complex.

"It's at Armthorpe; do you remember that we went to the pithead during the strike with provisions for the miners' wives? Now it's a country park, for walkers and joggers and cyclists where once there was a hive of industry. Armthorpe has changed from pit village to residential suburb in these past forty years. You'll come and see me when I've settled in, won't you Jess...I suppose this will be my final home, but at eighty and with a heart by-pass I really shouldn't be surprised that I need a bit of help, and those lovely young care girls will be sure to look after me well. An old fart like me doesn't mind being pushed about by those lassies, it's about the only advantage there is of getting old and infirm. Come and see me when Nick's next at the races and we'll talk over old times."

Chapter 35

Jess and Nick and Izzy were spending a weekend in the campervan. Jess wanted to explore Swaledale, the most northerly and remotest of the Yorkshire Dales. Passing a sign for Ravenseat, Jess remembered that this was where the Yorkshire Shepherdess of TV fame farmed, along with her husband and nine children. Jess had heard that the farm also did teas, so turned the van up the narrow moorland road.

At the head of the valley they found the farmhouse, reached by driving through a ford or by walking over a picturesque stone bridge. In front of the house was a catering van with the Shepherdess's eldest daughter serving cream teas. Jess ordered two, while Nick found a spare picnic table to which Izzy could be securely tied while they ate their scones. It was a beautiful sunny afternoon, and the scene was idyllic, with free range hens pecking in the grass and the sound of the stream murmuring in the background. Suddenly the peace was shattered by the noise of four jets passing overhead in formation, flying so low that Jess was afraid they might crash into the hill behind the farmhouse. The sound of the aircraft echoed around the valley and could be heard long after the jets had passed out of sight. It was a good thing that there was no filming taking place that afternoon, thought Jess. She went to use one of the portable toilets, leaving Nick in charge of Izzy, who was growing increasingly impatient at being fastened up while everyone else was tucking into cream teas. Returning after a few minutes, Jess was alarmed to discover that Izzy had somehow contrived to wriggle out of her harness and was joyously rampaging around the Yorkshire Shepherdess's tea garden, eyeing everyone's scones. It could only be a matter of moments before she snatched one from the plate of an unsuspecting diner; or worse still, spotted one of the free range hens..

Jess called to Izzy, and the dog ran over to her, with a typical Staffy grin on her face. Nick brought the harness, and Jess tightened the straps so that the dog could not escape again. Nick said Izzy had been anxious when Jess disappeared and had set off to look for her but had become distracted by the plates of food. A man appeared to clear away the tea things; Jess recognised him as the Shepherdess's husband. Then a school bus drew up and the three younger children of the family got out and made their way across the bridge. Jess hoped there would be enough scones left for their tea.

Jess and Nick shut Izzy in the campervan and set off for their campsite, in a riverside field a little further down the valley. There were a few other vehicles scattered about but plenty of room for everyone. After an evening stroll, Jess and Nick watched the moon rise over the hills; the stars appeared to shine more brightly here, well away from any light pollution. Jess fell asleep listening to the subdued sound of the river and the forlorn hooting of an owl in nearby woods.

Back home after the camping trip, Jess was pushing her trolley through the fruit and veg section in Asda when she glimpsed Ben the librarian and Film Club host, apparently heading in the opposite direction towards the fresh fish counter. Jess recalled how in former times, at the height of her crush, she might well have hastened after him, in an unseemly trolley dash round the store. As it was, Jess stayed on course and was choosing some leeks when she became aware of someone standing beside her. Looking up, she found that it was Ben, explaining that he was about to take early retirement from the library and that the Film Club would regrettably have to close, as he had not been able to persuade any of his colleagues to take it on.

"Oh that's a shame!" said Jess, adding "Of course, I hope you have a happy retirement. Do you have any immediate plans?"

Ben said that there were a number of things he must get done in the house but he had an idea for a script, which now he should be able to find the time to write. Jess wished him good luck, and then gave Ben some news of her own. She was about to visit Australia. After saving for many years, she had at last managed to accrue sufficient money to take a tour of some of the principle sites, finishing in Melbourne, where Tess and George, old friends from her university days, lived. Ben's eyes widened. "Australia! I've never been...well please avoid Hanging Rock, we don't want you to mysteriously disappear, like those girls in the film. Be very careful where you choose to picnic."

Jess assured him that she would be cautious about al fresco eating, although she was more afraid of venomous spiders than being mysteriously spirited away. She explained that the tour had an expert guide who would no doubt be well aware of all potential dangers and her friends had lived in Australia for many years, so far without mishap, so could be trusted to keep her safe.

"Anyway, I'd better let you get on. I'll put pictures of my trip on Facebook, do look at them if you are interested." Jess gathered up her leeks, Ben smiled, then headed off to complete his shopping.

Jess was making leek and potato soup when Nick appeared with a bag of dirty washing and began loading Jess's machine before disappearing upstairs. Nick had done his usual trick of leaving his phone downstairs, and glancing at the screen, Jess noted that Latin Sensations were again wishing to contact him. Jess was reminded that she had worrying information about the agency. Nick realised that he was without his phone and hurried down to retrieve it.

"Nick, you know that Latin Sensations doesn't have a very good write-up; it only gets one star out of five and several men have complained that the women aren't really the glamorous girls people might think they are, but are simply employees hired to write these messages to subscribers. The pictures might well be of models. It's possible that Paola may not be looking for a British boyfriend at all."

"Of course she's genuine! **Some** men may have had a bad experience with the women on the site but I've been really lucky, because I've got a lovely one! Anyway, the happy men wouldn't bother to leave a review, they'd be too busy enjoying themselves with their girls; it's only people who want to complain that ever write these comments!" Nick indignantly snatched up his phone and rushed away before Jess could say anything further.

It had been agreed that Nick should look after Izzy while Jess was in Australia. The date for her departure was rapidly approaching, she had sorted out her tickets and visa, and stocked up with Izzy's favourite brand of dog food. Jess's flight was booked from Manchester to Sydney via Abu Dhabi, arriving early in the morning, and she had arranged to spend the first day with her friend Maria before joining the organised tour group in the evening.

Jess's only worry was that she had been told she would have to share a room with another woman. She hoped the unknown roommate would be easy to get on with. Then a thought struck her. The local paper, the *Berringden Bugle*, had recently featured an item about someone from Berringden Brow who self-identified as female and had been sent to a women's prison, whereupon this person had raped some of the vulnerable inmates. Apparently, biological sex was not deemed as significant as self-identified gender these days. The rapist had later been removed to a men's jail, but the damage had been done and the effect on the victims would very probably be long-lasting.

Upon reading this, Jess began to worry that the person whose room she was to share during her trip might turn out to be a man who self-identified as a woman. She regretted not having paid the extra price for a single room, but it was now too late to alter the booking, since all the arrangements had been made. Nick pointed out that she might well be considered trans-phobic if she raised any objection to sharing with a someone self-identifying as female. He had heard that there was a law currently under discussion whereby in future anyone could apply to have their sex altered on their birth certificate without the requirement for medical intervention, so that if Jess found herself sharing a room with a person who self-identified as female there would be very little she could do about it. There was an organisation campaigning to protect safe spaces for women and girls so maybe Jess could join. Jess decided to follow the group, Fair Play for Women, on Facebook. It seemed that people such as the Berringden Brow rapist had simply chosen to say they were female without having had a medical consultation, hormone treatment or surgery, and they still had the wherewithal to abuse vulnerable women, so single-sex prisons, changing rooms and toilets were still needed.

Friends with experience of travel to Australia had told Jess that the journey was awful, and Jess was prepared for a tedious flight. She hated airports at the best of times and the security measures in place these days meant having to undress in the queue in front of everyone in an unseemly manner, in order to remove watch, belt, jacket, shoes and mobile phone. Clutching her trousers, afraid that they might fall down while she was obliged to be beltless, Jess watched anxiously as her belongings were put through the scanner. Fortunately, there was nothing which gave cause for concern, and Jess hastily reassembled herself, checking that all personal items had been returned to her.

Much to her annoyance, passengers for Sydney were obliged to repeat the entire performance at Abu Dhabi, although Jess could see no reason for this since she was simply in transit and surely the checks at Manchester should have been sufficient; after all, she had had no opportunity to acquire anything suspicious in the meantime. There was a further hour and a half before the onward flight and Jess tried to concentrate on her book, ignoring the grey and dusty airport surroundings. There was not a piece of greenery anywhere to be seen in the vicinity, the old phrase "the place where God left his shovel" sprang to mind, although Jess realised that Abu Dhabi must surely offer more to the visitor once away from the dreariness of the airport; she seemed to remember that one of the *Sex and the City* films had been made there. Visions of colourful souks and romantic desert scenery crossed her mind, but then she realised that her onward flight was boarding and so she made her way to the appointed gate. The next stop would be Sydney, and the start of her Australian adventure.

Chapter 36

It was a bright sunny morning as the plane landed in Sydney. Jess had been allocated an aisle seat, so had not had any opportunity to see the view as the plane descended. She collected her baggage and presented her passport for inspection, then proceeded to the taxi rank. Jess gave the driver the name of the hotel where the members of the tour were to assemble that evening and where her friend Maria had arranged to meet her at ten o'clock that morning.

A problem arose when Jess tried to use her her debit card to pay the taxi fare and it was declined. Jess had telephoned her bank before her departure to inform them that she was going to be travelling in Australia for three weeks, but the advisor told her that the bank no longer required or noted this information, since debit cards should work all over the world. Jess was not sure this was true, since on a previous trip to India she had found that her debit card had been declined on arrival at Delhi airport when she was trying to obtain Indian rupees. Luckily, Nick had been travelling with her, and his card had worked. In Udaipur, Nick's card was declined while Jess had no problem. They found throughout their journey that this often occurred, one or other of their cards was declined while another one worked, for no apparent reason, since there was money in both their accounts. However, Jess was now travelling alone with no immediate access to funds from her current account. She wondered what she could do but then remembered her credit card, which was accepted. Jess heaved a sigh of relief.

Jess approached the hotel desk and showed the receptionist her booking, only to be told that the room was not yet ready, since it was still very early. Jess sat in the reception area and soon dozed off. Eventually she was informed that her room was ready. She went upstairs, and found a standard featureless twin room. It was at the back of the building, and the window looked onto a brick courtyard. There was no sign yet of Jess's roommate. Jess had a quick shower and changed into clean clothes, then descended to the foyer where she was delighted to find her friend Maria waiting for her.

The two women had not seen each other since meeting on the Indian trip several years previously. Maria had thoughtfully bought a travel card for Jess, and they set out to explore the harbour area. Jess was thrilled to see the famous sights; as a child she had been given a card game called Round the World, which featured pictures of the most famous places to be found around the globe. The idea of the game was to collect a suite of pictures for the same continent. Young Jess had dreamed of visiting these far-off places, which at the time had not seemed possible for a girl whose travels at the time had taken her no further than Stonehenge; however, in her later years Jess had seen Table Mountain and the Taj Mahal, plus many of the game's featured European sights. Now she was seeing Sydney Harbour bridge and the Opera House and she could hardly believe it. Extensive travel had been the prerogative of the rich in Jess's childhood, but cheap air fares and reasonable pensions for some meant that more people could now reach exotic destinations. Travel had become more democratic.

In addition to the impressive structures and scenery, Jess was intrigued by the street performers, especially one elderly man dressed as Buddha who appeared to be balancing in mid-air in a crossed-leg sitting position supported only by a slender walking cane. Obviously it was some sort of trick but Jess could not fathom how it worked.

Maria had booked lunch on the top floor of the old Custom House, where the restaurant commanded a view over the harbour. The food was delicious and Maria generously insisted on paying. Jess knew that she was being thoroughly spoiled. The two women then spent a delightful afternoon in the Botanical Gardens, where the early Autumn plants were flourishing and a huge living wall of assorted greenery impressed Jess. There was also an interesting exhibition of various plants most useful to mankind. Jess was pleased to see kookaburras flying about among the trees. After a cup of tea, Jess realised that she must soon return to the hotel to meet the other members of her trip and discover with whom she was to share a room for the next fortnight, so they made their way back. Jess thanked Maria for a wonderful day and the two women hugged before parting. Jess then braced herself and went upstairs.

This was the moment of truth when she would discover if her roommate was a self-identifying female similar to the Berringden Brow prison rapist. Jess unlocked the door to be greeted by a smiling woman of about the same age as herself with fair wavy hair and glasses, busily hanging up her clothes in the wardrobe. The woman introduced herself as Heather. Jess returned her greeting. She was so pleased to find that she was sharing with someone who appeared to be the quintessential Englishwoman abroad that she sank down onto her bed, sighing with relief.

The tour group met in the hotel lounge at six o'clock. The leader was a young woman called Alice who came from Queensland. There were only seven people in the group, including a Canadian couple and three Americans - a couple and a single lady from Savannah. Heather and Jess were the only British guests. All were about retirement age. Alice briefly outlined the arrangements and itinerary, and then they all went for dinner. Jess did not need a large meal since she had enjoyed a sumptuous lunch with Maria. Her main concern was to find a cash machine which would accept her debit card. Fortunately, Alice was able to show her an ATM which worked.

Back at the hotel, Jess apologised to Heather for any snoring which might disturb her, although Heather assured her that she generally slept soundly; however she had brought earplugs as a precaution.

Chapter 37

The group spent the first full day exploring Sydney. Part of their tour was led by an Aboriginal woman who welcomed them with a traditional smudging ceremony, but unfortunately the scented smoke cloud set off Ellen, the Canadian lady's asthma. The day ended with a boat trip around the harbour, with supper and drinks. Everyone was obliged to have their photograph taken at sunset, clutching a glass of wine, with the bridge and Opera House in the background. It made for a striking picture, with the evening sky streaked with brilliant red. Alice said they had been very lucky with the weather. Just as they were returning to the shore, Jess was very pleased to notice a White

Ribbon emblem illuminated on one of the pillars of the bridge. She had done some voluntary work with the White Ribbon campaign back home in Berringden Brow; the charity works with men to raise awareness of issues surrounding domestic violence and invites them to pledge to work against violence to women and girls.

The next part of the trip took them to the tropical North-East, where they stayed near Four Mile Beach. Jess went for a walk along the sand, noting that there was only a limited area where it was safe to enter the water, because of the danger posed from sharks. Jess herself was not bothered about swimming, she had not learned to swim until she was twelve and she had never really enjoyed it. The open-air pool which was Tiverton Swimming Baths in the 1960s had not encouraged her to learn, since the water rarely rose above 54 degrees F, (11 degrees C). Indoor, heated baths had not arrived until after Jess had left the town. Jess was content to stroll, and then to sit on a log to admire the view and read. Later she wandered into the town and some bought postcards. She noticed a cafe offering free Wi-Fi, so decided to send a message to Nick and Izzy. The waiter gave her the internet access code. He had an unmistakable Manchester accent. Jess told him she lived not far from his home town, whereupon he replied that she was third person that morning to have said the same thing. There was evidently an influx of British Northerners at Four Mile Beach. He was coming to the end of his six-month stay, having worked throughout the Australian summer season. Of course, this being the southern hemisphere, the month of May was Autumn, and he would be returning home just as the British summer arrived.

That evening, Alice cooked a delicious barbeque and discussed arrangements for the following day's snorkeling trip. Everyone except Jess planned to go snorkeling, but Jess, with her dislike of swimming, had booked a less adventurous excursion in a glass bottomed boat. However, when it came to departure time, Jess's trip was cancelled due to rough seas. The snorkelers had already left, but soon Heather and the Canadian couple returned. They had gone out on the boat, but the engine had failed, so another boat had been sent to fetch them. Meanwhile, the sea had become extremely rough, so they were given the choice of returning or continuing with the trip on the new boat. The three Americans chose to carry on, while the others opted to join Jess on a visit to a local animal sanctuary.

"What a strange-looking creature! exclaimed Heather, as they caught sight of a cassowary, and indeed, it did look like something out of Jurassic Park. Ellen's husband, Dylan, was taking lots of photographs of the tame kangaroos. Jess wondered just what had brought them to the rescue centre, and learned from the information board that most had been orphaned at an early age. They watched the koalas being fed eucalyptus and wondered if they would be lucky enough to spot these animals in the wild later on in their trip.

The following day the party arrived in Cairns, where they decided to find a Chinese restaurant at which diners cooked their own food at the table. Cynthia, the single American lady, had heard about it. Each person chose a variety of soup and what they would like to eat with it; the soup bowl was placed on a heated plate and thin strips of delicious meat and vegetables were then quickly cooked in the hot soup. After their interesting meal they strolled along the seafront, watching flocks of long-billed birds searching for food on the shore.

At Mossman Gorge the following day an Aboriginal man named Tom led them on a guided walk, demonstrating how the various wild plants could be used for food, building shelters, making weapons and even to create washing suds. The jungle was able provide everything the rainforest Aboriginal people required. Jess had always thought of Australia as being mostly desert, with a temperate coastal fringe to the South and a Mediterranean-type strip in the West. She forgot that this part of the country was definitely in the tropics. As if to reinforce the point, they were taken in a cable car over the canopy at Karanda. Jess and Heather shared a rather cramped gondola with Dylan and Ellen, but Jess was rather unnerved by Dylan's obsession with taking photographs. He kept standing up to snap the view, although Jess would have preferred him to sit still and simply admire the scenery as they swung over the tree-tops. Finally he lost his balance and fell towards Jess's corner of the gondola which lurched alarmingly; they all shouted at Dylan to sit down and thankfully he was persuaded to stay in his seat for the remainder of the journey. Jess alighted with great relief, since cable cars were not really her preferred form of transport. She was always anxious that the system might break down and she would be stuck for hours in mid-air, with no facilities. Jess had previously travelled in cable cars in Madeira, Austria and Italy without mishap, but the underlying anxiety was always there.

After inspecting the dramatic gorge and looking around the town of Karanda the return journey was by train, which suited Jess much better. She had seen Michael Portillo on one of his *Great Railway Journeys* travelling on the Karanda line, and was very pleased to be doing the same trip. The coaches were old-fashioned with open windows and the train comprised so many of them that at one point, where the track rounded a sharp curve, the front coaches could be seen from the rear ones. Back in Cairns, Jess's companions were heading out to yet another exotic restaurant, but Jess felt that she would simply like fish and chips. She walked along the seafront until she came to a cafe she had noticed the previous evening. Despite the friendliness of her travelling companions, Jess was glad of the opportunity to be alone for a while. She had postcards to write and a book to read, and was enjoying her relaxing evening and traditional seaside meal. The sight of a passing Staffy made her rather homesick but a text message from Nick assured her that he and Izzy were fine.

Chapter 38

Leaving Cairns, the group headed for Uluru, which was the sight to which Jess had been looking forward the most. It was naturally very hot in the desert after the pleasant temperature at the coast, and they discovered to their annoyance that there were clouds of flies buzzing everywhere. Everyone rushed out to buy black net veils, which when placed over bush hats, afforded some measure of protection. While Jess had of course heard about Uluru (formerly known as Ayer's Rock) she was surprised to find that there was another distinctive red sandstone landform close by - Kata Tjuta (previously called The Olgas) a striking cluster of ancient rocks in a remote basin.

They checked into the hotel, which was really more like a hostel, with little chalets dotted around a campus and communal cooking facilities. This arrangement suited Jess better than the more sophisticated establishments at which they had been staying, and reminded her of her trip to Africa, with the bush scenery and preponderance of young back-packing types among the guests. There was a more up-market hotel next door with beautiful gardens full of colourful blooms The resort area is situated outside the National Park so that accommodation is away from the sacred ground round Uluru.

That first evening Jess discovered that everyone except herself had opted for an expensive fine-dining experience under the stars, and coaches were on hand to collect people from the various hotels. Jess had chosen a more modest adventure, an evening's star-gazing out in the desert, and was planning a simple omelette for her tea, with eggs bought at the resort supermarket and cooked in the hostel kitchen. Not wishing to risk travelling with eggs in her luggage, Jess cooked all six, so that there was far too much food for her. All the other hostellers using the kitchen seemed to have plenty to eat. Then Jess thought that the staff on the reception desk might not have had their supper, so she took a plateful of omelette through to the front hall. The young man on duty accepted the food gladly.

"This is the first time any of the guests has ever cooked for us!" exclaimed the receptionist. "Hey, Jim!" he called to his colleague. "Come and get some tucker this kind lady has made. We're on duty 'til eleven tonight so it will late before we're getting any more grub."

Jim emerged from the office, and setting the plate on the counter Jess handed the men a couple of forks and left them to it. She was due to meet the astronomy group leader outside the hotel for the evening's session. The star-gazing group walked a little distance into the bush, away from the lighted buildings. The leader and another man were carrying a couple of elaborate-looking telescopes which they proceeded to assemble in a clearing. Jess had previously seen the Southern night sky in Africa, but had forgotten the names of most of the constellations, except of course for the Southern Cross. The stars appeared so very much brighter and closer then did their Northern counterparts in Berringden Brow, which was of course at a much higher latitude and affected by the light pollution of the nearby conurbations. Jess enjoyed looking through the powerful telescopes at the beautiful images; the brilliantly-shining moon appeared to be almost within touching distance.

Heather arrived back at the hotel after the sumptuous open-air meal, and she and Jess exchanged news on how their evenings had gone. The pair found that they got on very well, so that it was absolutely no hardship to share a room. Heather admitted that she had initial reservations about sharing with a stranger, but these had all vanished on meeting Jess; in her turn Jess was emboldened to express her fear of being obliged to room with a man who self-identified as female and her relief on meeting Heather that first evening in Sydney. Heather erupted into gales of laughter and declared that she would be dining out on this story for years to come. Jess was the only person she knew who could have come up with such an outlandish idea, and she had better buy a copy of Jess's book...

They set their alarm clocks for an early start, in order to watch the dawn over Uluru. The desert looked almost grey when they arrived, but soon the rising sun brought vivid colour and sound to the area; the experience was well worth the effort of getting up so very early. There seemed to be a plethora of hidden creatures living in the bush, all greeting the day with twittering and chirping. Jess learned later, on a trip to a local visitor and craft centre, that there were in fact 77 recorded species of reptiles and amphibians in the national park and 178 species of bird. However, what interested her most were the wonderful Aboriginal artworks produced by the centre users. Jess bought a packet of colourful postcards and a book written by a local woman as a gift for her friend Tess, with whom she was soon to stay.

That evening, Jess, Heather and Cynthia had chosen to visit the Field of Light. "An area the size of seven football pitches containing 50,000 stems crowned with radiant frosted glass spheres of different hues," read Jess from the guidebook. "It sounds magical!" Indeed it was, and none of them had previously seen anything similar. Great swathes of yellow, pink, blue, purple, red, white and green lights covered the area of the installation, glowing in the desert night. Without a guided tour, visitors were simply allowed to wander at will along the maze of paths through the sea of lights. The coach driver had warned them they must be back at the gate by 8.30. It would be easy to lose track of time in such surroundings, so Jess made sure to keep an eye on her watch. As 8.30 approached the three women made their way along a path leading to the exit, only to be met by a group of anxious-looking people coming in the opposite direction.

"You're going the wrong way!" shouted one man.

"No we're not!" exclaimed Jess, for it did indeed seem that the exit was getting nearer. They had been provided with a map, but it was not easy to make out the small print in the subdued light. Cynthia shone her mobile phone torch onto the diagram, and confirmed that they were indeed going in the right direction. However, confusingly, it turned out that this path did not lead directly to the exit, but meandered round various clumps of lights, so that at one point it seemed that they were actually walking away from the gate. They eventually made their way to the edge of the field and arrived at the exit with some relief, just in time to board the coach. Jess wondered if the people they had encountered had managed to find their way out in time, or whether one bus would have to stay behind to pick up the stragglers. No-one would choose to spend the night in the field, however beautiful, for who knew what snakes and creepy-crawlies might emerge once all the tourists left and the rightful inhabitants had the place to themselves until the next morning?

It was hotter than ever the next day and Jess really did not want to walk all the way around the base of Uluru. The indefatigable Americans set off at a brisk pace, carrying several bottles of water. National Park rules stipulated that everyone should drink one litre of water per hour, wear a broad-brimmed hat, stout shoes, and use sunscreen. Jess, along with Ellen, chose a more relaxing stroll to admire the rock art. Returning to the rendez-vous point, Jess was upset to discover that people were climbing the rock; there were notices requesting tourists not to do this, and to respect the fact that this was a sacred place to the Aboriginal people. Tour guide Alice said that climbing Uluru was shortly to be made illegal since polite requests had failed to deter thoughtless and insensitive climbers.

That evening brought a sunset picnic. Alice arranged sparkling wine and tasty bites on one of the wooden tables set up at some distance from Uluru, where the changing colours could best be admired. Jess thought this must surely be one of the wonders of the world. She was sad to be leaving Uluru, the highlight of her Australian adventure so far, but Melbourne and a week's visit to her friends Tess and George beckoned. She and Heather hugged and promised to stay in touch.

Chapter 39

Jess's friend Tess had been the map curator at the Geography Department of Leeds University when Jess was a student; Jess had then had a summer holiday job, assisting Tess to reorganise the map collection, and the two had become friends. Some of the old plans of the Yorkshire Coalfield looked as though they had indeed been taken down a mine, so dirty and illegible had they become, so that Tess and Jess had resorted to scrubbing the linen maps with Handy Andy. Jess also babysat for Tess and George's young son, now grown up with his own wife and child. Work had taken the family overseas, first to France where Jess had visited them in the 1970s and on to Australia. George had many relatives back in the UK, so Jess had been able to see her friends on their visits home. This trip to visit them in Australia was a long-held dream

The next few days passed happily. In addition to sight-seeing Tess took Jess to lunch with the ladies from her gym and also to a coffee morning at the library in the suburb where she and George lived. Like Jess, Tess was keen on discovering bargains in charity shops (known as Op Shops in Australia) and Jess found a pretty dish for Zofia. She had bought Alex a boomerang at Uluru, and some herbal tea and Australian honey for Tom. For Nick, Jess found a true story book about a cross-continental car journey in the 1930s.

Tess and George had a swimming pool in their garden, and Tess swam every morning. Jess was persuaded to go in once, but found the autumnal water rather chilly. The pool was left unheated during the winter; Tess was convinced of the health benefits of cold water dips but George was less keen and preferred to swim in summer.

Jess really enjoyed wandering around Melbourne, with its colourful street art and busy little alleyways full of enticing restaurants, shops and cafes, its extensive market, beautiful Botanical Gardens and riverside walks. She took the free tram which plied a circular route around the periphery of the centre, enabling people to hop on and off at will. Jess discovered a small piece of Yorkshire, Captain Cook's house which had been brought all the way from the UK and rebuilt in the corner of a park. Everything inside, plus the surrounding cottage garden, was as it would have been in James Cook's parents' time.

On her last full day, Tess and George took Jess to a nearby Sculpture Park, next to the sea and with wonderful views, where she was amazed to recognise something else from Yorkshire - an installation previously seen at the Sculpture Park at Bretton Hall. This depicted a galloping horse on a LED screen, and Jess wondered if it could perhaps have been a copy of the Yorkshire one or the original shipped halfway round the world. She resolved to check online.

Tess and George drove Jess to the airport for her long flight home, which included a tedious five hour wait at Abu Dhabi. Jess was of course looking forward to getting back home to Nick and her beloved Izzy, but sad to be leaving her friends and their beautiful country. Izzy gave Jess a rapturous welcome on her return. All was well at home, and Nick had remembered to water the plants. Jess was so tired after her gruelling flight that she went straight to bed. It would take several days for her to get back into the routine of life in Berringden Brow, and meanwhile she had dozens of photographs to sort out and post on Facebook.

Chapter 40

Awakening after a long sleep, Jess had a surprise waiting for her. Alex sent a picture of a grey blob, which Jess initially could not make out until a clearer picture followed, of a foetus lying on its back. It was a hospital scan of the baby Alex and Zofia were expecting in the autumn! Jess was delighted and thought she would be a traditional granny, so went to look out her knitting needles.

Now that Jess was safely home and able to resume looking after Izzy, it would soon be time for Nick to embark his overseas trip. He had booked a flight to El Dorado airport in Colombia, where he was intending to meet his beautiful young girlfriend, Paola. He had armed himself with a comprehensive selection of Spanish phrasebooks and guidebooks to South America and felt quite prepared for a later-life adventure. Nick was undeterred by any reservations as to the wisdom of this journey expressed online or by Jess; he was single-mindedly intent on meeting Paola and insisted that nothing would stop him from going to Medellin.

Jess's main anxiety stemmed from the fact that Nick had still not spoken to Paola directly and their text conversations were always mediated by the introduction agency, since those were apparently their rules. Nick did not have Paola's surname or her address; he was relying on the hope that once he arrived in Medellin, she would emerge from behind the screen of the introduction agency and they would fall into each other's arms.

Frank shook his head when Jess told him about Nick's plans.

"There's no fool like an old fool! What's the age difference? Forty years! It all seems so unlikely doesn't it... A Colombian beauty is content with a long-distance romance with a man old enough to be her grandfather, spurning all offers from younger chaps close at hand... Pull the other one!"

Tom said that Nick could still have a very good time in Colombia, whether or not Paola agreed to meet him, which he thought unlikely. After all, it was a beautiful country, but it would be much better for Nick to arrange to join an escorted tour, especially in view of his propensity for getting into overseas scrapes. Every pimp, tart and gangster for miles around seemed to home in when Nick arrived on foreign soil, as evidenced by his various adventures in Pakistan, Africa and Indonesia. Jess still shuddered to recall Nick's trip to the North-West frontier in the lawless tribal area of Pakistan, disguised in traditional robes and improbably described by his companions as being deaf-mute, in order that no-one they met upon the way should be surprised at his lack of communication. Nick had been photographed in his disguise, toting a Kalashnikov, the property of his hosts; not the typical holiday snap brought back to Berringden Brow from an overseas trip.

Then again, it was one thing for Jess to have wired Nick additional funds as she had been urgently requested to do during his Indonesian escapade, but she would certainly not be in a position to raise sufficient money to ransom Nick if he were to be kidnapped in Colombia. Nick needed a minder whenever he ventured overseas. The news on the World Service, to which Jess tuned in at night, did not make for encouraging listening. There was civil unrest in many Colombian towns and cities, with unions threatening strikes, and rioting by disgruntled workers. Nick assured Jess that Paola reported Medellin as being completely safe.

"But the Foreign Office advice is against all but essential visits to Colombia, so won't that invalidate your travel insurance?"

Nick was completely deaf to Jess's prevarications. Jess was exasperated by the fact that Nick, who had spent his career giving advice to thousands, ably assisting people to navigate a path through various complex rules and regulations, was so dismissive of her sensible admonitions. He was determined to see Paola despite all notes of caution from friends and warnings from officialdom. Nothing would stop him, and he ignored all entreaties to postpone his trip until the situation in Colombia became more settled.

Nick's flight was within a few hundred miles of its destination when the Captain announced that local Air Traffic Controllers at El Dorado airport had mounted a lightening strike and that the country's airspace was now closed. Their plane would be diverted to Panama City, the nearest available airport. This announcement was greeted with consternation by the passengers, but given the rather alarming news about Bogota there was absolutely nothing else to be done.

On arrival in Panama, the anxious travellers collected their baggage and were shepherded into a room where they were met by a local hotel manager who explained that he had been instructed by the British Consul to escort them to his hotel. A woman approached Nick, whom he recognised as Jasmine, a client from his advice centre days. He had not noticed her at the airport or on the plane but she had apparently just seen him passing by on his way from the toilet. Jasmine explained that she had been intending to visit a cousin who lived in Cali. Nick said he had tried to send a message to his friend in Medellin, but had so far received no reply. Communications to Colombia were becoming difficult, hardly surprising given all that was going on. However, Jasmine said she had just managed to get through to her cousin, who warned her not to attempt to cross into Colombia, since the country was now in lockdown with armed police patrolling the streets and shooting at anyone who broke the curfew. The countryside was said to be a tinderbox waiting to explode. Nick then tried to send another message to Paola, but it was returned as Undelivered. It seemed there was nothing for it but to do as instructed and board one of the buses now leaving for the hotel.

When they arrived, the manager's harassed-looking assistant passed through the crowd gathered in the foyer, issuing dockets for rooms. Seeing Nick and Jasmine together he mistakenly assumed that they were a couple and consequently gave them a docket for an ensuite twin room. Nick ran after him to explain that he and Jasmine were not partners but by the time he managed to get the man's attention all the rooms had been allocated so they went upstairs to find theirs.

"Well, I suppose we'll just have to make the best of it, after all, it won't be for long; I imagine we will have to get a return flight as soon as possible now Colombia is no go," sighed Jasmine.

"I've not come all this way simply to go straight back home!" said Nick. "We can at least take the opportunity to look around Panama."

Jasmine did not seem certain that this was really a very good idea. "Surely we had better do what the British Consul advises? He's sent that message saying stay in the hotel and await further instructions."

"I'll discuss it with him when he comes to see us later."

By the time the British Consul had arrived at the hotel for a meeting with the stranded travellers Nick had checked online and found that there was a cruise ship leaving Panama the next day for the UK via the Azores and Madeira. The ship was on the final leg of a Round the World voyage, having sailed through the Mediterranean, Suez Canal, Red Sea, Indian Ocean, across the Pacific visiting various islands en route, and finally transited the Panama Canal to rejoin the Atlantic Ocean. However, the Consul was dubious about Nick's suggestion of sailing home.

"These cruise ships usually have a full complement of passengers, and I doubt they will be able to take anyone extra at this stage. But leave it with me, and I'll get back to you."

As good as his word, the Consul rang Nick the following morning.

"You're in luck; it seems they do after all have a spare cabin, because one of the passengers died while crossing the Pacific. His body was repatriated and his wife flew home from Fiji. The ship sails this evening, and you can get a taxi to the port at four o'clock. The Panamanian authorities have given permission for you to leave the hotel to go sightseeing this morning; there is no visa requirement for British visitors who have arrived by air, you just need a credit card and to have made arrangements for onward travel."

Nick and Jasmine spent the next day looking around the Old Town of Panama City, before taking a taxi to the Port, where they boarded the huge ship which was to take them back to the UK. They discovered that the unfortunate deceased passenger and his wife had occupied a luxury cabin with a balcony. Nick had paid for the voyage with his credit card, and Jasmine promised to reimburse him for her share when they returned home. Meanwhile they could look forward to almost two weeks of cruising, with stops at the Azores and Madeira.

Nick had repeatedly tried to contact Paola, without success. The situation in Colombia was still very volatile. As an afterthought, he had emailed Jess, explaining the change of plan. He knew she would have kept abreast of the news and would expect him to be returning home on the flight with the other stranded Brits. Nick was pleased to have been able to salvage something from his trans-Atlantic trip; he was concerned as to what might have become of Paola, but there was nothing he could do, with the borders closed and all communications down. Now he had Jasmine for company; of course, she was not a beauty like Paola, but she was certainly pleasant enough. Nick set out to explore the ship, leaving Jasmine reading a book on their balcony as the liner majestically sailed from the harbour.

Chapter 41

Jess received Nick's email with relief. She had anxiously followed the news about the unrest in Colombia, and had imagined Nick caught in crossfire and injured while searching the streets for Paola. Nick's journey had appeared to be the very wildest of wild goose chases, with no definite arrangements and not even an address for Paola. Their messages had all been via the introduction agency and cost Nick a certain number of credits, which was no doubt how the agency made its money. Now it seemed it would not be possible for him to meet Paola, if indeed she actually existed; but he had met up with a woman from Berringden called Jasmine, who turned out to be a former advice centre client of his. Jess cast her mind back to when she had been Nick's assistant, and she did indeed remember a sensible lady named Jasmine visiting the advice centre accompanied by a number of small children, who would by now be grown up. So all was well, and Nick would have the pleasure of seeing the Azores, the lush mid-Atlantic islands which Alex had once visited on a Tall Ships sailing expedition. A lad from the local organisation dealing with disaffected young people where Alex had a placement had dropped out, and Alex, being at the time the only youngster of the group with a current passport, had taken his place at the last minute. The trip was funded by a bursary, so Jess had not been required to pay anything towards Alex's adventure. Jess reflected that Alex's circumstances had in some respects been similar to Nick's present situation, with an opportunity to travel to the Azores having unexpectedly arisen. She wondered if it would be three times lucky and she would one day find herself in a position to visit the beautiful islands at short notice, but doubted that she would be so fortunate.

Jess and Izzy were taking their customary walk through the woods when they encountered someone coming towards them pushing a pram on an overgrown stretch of the path. Jess stood aside, to allow the pram to pass; she then noticed that it was being pushed by her erstwhile neighbour, Ryan. Jess stopped to admire the baby.

"Hello Ryan, is this little girl an addition? What's her name?"

"This is Summer," said Ryan, proudly.

"Well, congratulations, she's lovely."

Following Ryan's sudden departure from the house round the corner, it seemed that he had got together with a girlfriend and started a family. He certainly looked much happier than before. Jess was very pleased for him. As for her own family, Zofia's recent scan had revealed that Jess's eagerly expected grandchild was to be a girl.

Alex and Zofia were having a barbeque at the allotment. It was the first of August, Yorkshire Day, and also the Celtic celebration of Lughnasa, marking the beginning of the harvest season, when first fruits are picked. Everyone from the surrounding allotments was bringing a contribution of produce. The allotment was looking lovely, with a riot of fruit and vegetables growing everywhere and colourful sweet peas and nasturtiums climbing the fences. Alex had built a huge bonfire and Zofia was busy cooking steaks, with vegetarian sausages for those who preferred not to eat meat, while various dogs were watching her every move. Cans of beer were keeping cool in the pond and Alex's special home-brewed sparkling elderflower wine was flowing liberally. Tom arrived with a young woman whom he introduced as Helen who it turned out had read Jess's book, so the two were soon chatting happily. Then Jasmine came with her youngest child, a teenage girl who offered to assist Zofia with the food. Jasmine said that when things were calmer in Colombia she might try again to visit her cousin, but Nick had heard nothing at all from Paola, and seemed, for the moment at least, to be content enough in Berringden Brow, although Jess had recently noticed some travel brochures for the Far East on his bedside table...

A glorious sunset lit up the sky as Zofia handed round the food.

"Well," said Jess, passing Nick a can of beer retrieved from the pond. "You wanted an adventure, and you got one, although not quite what you expected. More of a wild goose chase really. But you can still have adventures, they need just a bit more planning and a proper response from someone at your intended destination. And maybe take me with you next time. This 'innocent abroad' thing is wearing a bit thin; you always seem to run into some sort of difficulty - tangling with the Mujahedeen, falling prey to pimps and their call girls, civil unrest - wherever there's danger, you'll find it, or it seems to find you! We're old age pensioners and I'm about to become a grandmother, so maybe we should in future stick to Saga trips and settle for a quiet life."

"But I don't feel old!" exclaimed Nick. "And I'm absolutely not ready to be a Saga customer! Who wants a quiet life - it certainly doesn't appeal to me! And on days like these surely it's better to embrace life with all its opportunities, rather than hide away from it. After all, what do we have to lose?"

Also by Jill Robinson:

Berringden Brow - Memoirs of a Single Parent with Crush

Introducing Jess and her friends the struggling yet still optimistic middle-aged women of a Pennine village, who find themselves coping with stroppy teenage kids, ageism, sexism, lookism, sizeism... scanning the personal columns in search of that rare eligible man without hypochondria, a live-in mother, multiple allergies, a preference for playing with toy soldiers or a penchant for sex in public places. But whenever it all gets too much for Jess, she can always escape into the library.

"this richly enjoyable, funny and humane read." Sue Limb

Sons and Lodgers

All Jess wants is a quiet life. all her friends want is somewhere to stay...

Jess feels her serenity slipping as she struggles with teenage tantrums, men's mid-life crises, dope, dogs, refugees, rampant plants, rough sleepers in the shed and bureaucrats on the doorstep - and she is rapidly running out of floor space.

Continuing the every-day story of life in Berringden Brow, a sequel to the hilarious *Memoirs of a Single Parent with a Crush*

A Place Like This

So many people find their way to the advice centre - asylum seekers, debtors, a trafficked young woman, a heart-broken husband, a man with evil spirits in the house. Jess tries her best to help everyone, while contending with the erratic life-style of her son who has embraced freeganism and plastered Hebden Bridge with graffiti. Meanwhile, friends also need her support - but who will help Jess?

Life's Rich Tapestry

Working on a research project collecting the life histories of care home residents, Jess encounters a variety of people eager to tell their stories, including a melancholic mariner, a disillusioned cleric, a love-sick octogenarian and the Yorkshire Ripper's former newsagent. Meanwhile, Jess reflects how her own life has led her from running around the Wishing Tree to chasing errant peacocks down the back streets of Berringden Brow.

Then she finds herself at a seaside Folk Festival, chaperoning a troupe of 45 Koreans...

The New Forty

Now retired, Jess finds that many people are anxious to call upon her for assistance. Jess is anxious to help in whatever way she can, but discovers that her well-intentioned actions are not always appropriate or appreciated.

Meanwhile, a number of interesting opportunities present themselves - stewarding at Glastonbury, appearing on a tea-time quiz show, volunteering with a children's charity in Romania and distributing prizes at a writing competition in a haunted barn. Then she finds herself on a storm-tossed cruise ship in the middle of the Baltic, in company with an ageing debutante and a young cage-fighter.

"An entertaining series of small-town oddness..."

The Rainy Season

1960s small town Devonshire, where things are far from swinging and Jess struggles with the double standard whereby daughters must do housework while their brothers go out to play and Saturday girls receive threepence per hour less than their male counterparts. A married woman's income is treated as belonging to her husband and she requires a male guarantor simply to rent a television set. There is no protection from Domestic Violence, and Jess shares a barricaded bedroom with her depressed mother against the rages of her alcoholic father, who does not believe in education for girls. Jess longs to grow up and escape, but it seems to be taking such an awfully longtime... meanwhile the pace of social change is quickening, even in sleepy market towns, with abortion law reform, the decriminalisation of homosexuality, divorce law reform, the lowering of the age of majority from 21 to eighteen (an innovation detested by many parents, including Jess's) - and then the Pill becomes available.

A poignant and widely-praised memoir of a time - seemingly light years away in terms of attitudes and social conditions - yet still within living memory.

5 stars on Amazon, 4 stars on Goodreads

For further details please see the Berringden Brow Facebook page or contact Jill on berringdenbrow@hotmail.co.uk